THE HERON STAYED

ALSO BY JANE S. CREASON

Fiction

When the War Came to Hannah

THE HERON STAYED

Jane S. Creason

Trafford

Order this book online at www.trafford.com
or email orders@trafford.com

Most Trafford titles are also available at major online book retailers.

© Copyright 2011 Jane S. Creason.
All rights reserved. No part of this publication may be reproduced, stored
in a retrieval system, or transmitted, in any form or by any means, electronic,
mechanical, photocopying, recording, or otherwise, without
the written prior permission of the author.

This novel is a work of fiction. Names, characters, places, and incidents are
products of the author's imagination. All characters are fictional, and any
similarity to persons living or dead is entirely coincidental.

Printed in the United States of America.

ISBN: 978-1-4269-6179-3 (sc)
ISBN: 978-1-4269-6180-9 (e)

Trafford rev. 04/05/2011

North America & international
toll-free: 1 888 232 4444 (USA & Canada)
phone: 250 383 6864 • fax: 812 355 4082

Dedicated to those who have stayed by me

Don
Todd and Valerie, Lockie and Chris
Jackie, Cameron, Maddie, and Katie

Chapter 1

Sometimes late at night when the wind-blown trees tossed playful dim shadows on the sloping ceiling of his small upstairs room, Chap lay wide awake, thinking about his life, which was as predictable as a heartbeat shown on one of those hospital machines with the line that jogs up and down. Thud-thud, thud-thud, thud-thud, thud-thud.

Not that his life was ordinary with an older sister, who was like a mother, and a father, who was retired from the army and who rarely ventured from his den, so involved he was in writing a book about war—a book he never talked about but one that had consumed his time and energy for years. The closed door to his father's den was a normal part of Chap's existence along with the big square two-story house, set back from First Woods Road in a small grassy clearing in the Indiana woods.

Chap liked his time alone in the woods, his sister was his best friend, and he loved to read and write. None of that made his life ordinary. But he was content for the most part with his quiet existence. Thud-thud. Thud-thud. The patient, white-draped and still, was stable and doing fine. That was Chap—stable and doing fine. Get up-go to school-come home-go to bed. Get up-go to school-come home-go to bed. Even the weekends and the summers had their own settled routines that hardly disturbed the even pattern of the line.

Then shortly before his sophomore year started at Riverwoods High School, there was a blip, and the line flew off the chart.

* * *

One muggy August afternoon, Chap ate his usual lunch of a bologna and Swiss cheese sandwich—no lettuce, no mayo—before hiking the familiar path through the woods to a stony bluff overlooking Wandering River. Appropriately named by early settlers, the river flowed from the east into the area around Riverwoods, then angled sharply north, then almost straight west, and then south to form a three-sided box around the small city of about thirty thousand. But the river wasn't done wandering yet. After leaving Riverwoods, it bent west again for about ten miles and then north, making another three-sided box around the gently rolling, wooded hills where Chap lived.

That day the Church Rock at the top of the bluff was warm and inviting, high above the river, which appeared flat and unmoving, more like glass than water as it reflected the sprinkle of puffy clouds above. Chap sat awhile, letting the sun toast his back, before moving from the edge of the bluff into the shade beneath a gigantic hard maple tree that would turn from late-summer dusty green to blazing orange in a couple of months. Opening Steinbeck's *The Red Pony Stories*, he was soon immersed in the joy and pain of Jody's life.

* * *

Several hours later when his stomach began to growl too loudly and too often to be ignored, Chap stuck a blade of grass between two pages of the book and headed downhill for the ten-minute hike home. When he stepped onto the scuffed gray steps leading to the screened porch that stretched across the back of the house, he knew even before opening the door into the big, airy kitchen that something was different. It was the smell of warm cinnamon.

Lori, his twenty-three-year-old sister, was standing at the counter, wearing her favorite green apron with white button eyes and a smiling red rickrack mouth, which their father had suggested she create—once her tears had dried—to cover the slit caused when her scissors slipped as she was finishing her first sewing project for ninth grade home economics. Lori was swaying to the music from an old boxy radio that sat on top of the refrigerator, hands deep in the meatloaf she was mixing.

"Hey, Little Brother, it's good food tonight," she said, smiling.

"Why are you home so early?" he asked, peeking into the oven at the bubbling apple pie.

"I've got big news. I'll tell you about it during supper," she said, pushing a strand of dark curly hair away from her temple with the back of her hand and smearing the flour streak on her cheek. "How 'bout you folding the laundry while I finish getting this into the oven?"

"How 'bout I don't?"

"Oh," she said, moving to the sink to wash her hands. "Defying authority, are we?"

She whirled around, shooting water at Chap from the sprayer. And the war was on. She shot bursts of water at him. He dodged and ducked, but the sprayer's supple black hose allowed her to take deadly aim. Both were laughing.

Finally, Chap raised his arms. "I surrender," he yelled, water dripping off his face and onto his soaked shirt. "You win. I'll fold the laundry."

"That's better," she said.

Lori replaced the sprayer in its hole by the faucet. Picking up the casserole dish, she moved towards the oven.

"Oh, and can you get me the sponge mop from the basement? For some reason, there's water all over the floor."

"You're pathetic," he said with a grin.

"Just get the mop," she said, her eyes wide and insistent but her mouth ready to smile.

* * *

Later as the pie cooled on the counter and Lori stirred cheese into the potatoes, Chap carried the good china plates with the delicate pink flowers around the edges and the crystal goblets they used for special occasions to the oak table in the corner of the kitchen. Long ago the table had been an elongated oval with two leaves and many chairs, then later a shorter oval with one leaf and fewer chairs, and finally a circle with only three chairs.

Their father always sat closest to the door that led to the formal dining room, where they never dined, through the living room, where they rarely sat, and back to his den. He generally appeared after the food was placed on the table, then disappeared before either Lori or Chap had finished eating.

Over the past several years, their father had become so quiet, so totally immersed in his writing that Chap could hardly remember the old days when he'd prepared himself for suppertime conversation—beginning way back when there were more than three chairs around the table.

Mealtime then had generally been a serious affair but certainly not a quiet one. Chap's earliest memories included his father asking all of his sisters what they'd learned that day. The first time Chap had reported on his academic progress was when he was a kindergartener. As usual, each of his sisters had been asked, and Chap had listened attentively, something else their father expected.

Suddenly, his father turned and said, "And you, Son, what did you learn today?"

In the hush that followed and with all those eyes staring at him, every thought of the numbers he could count and the letters he could print vanished.

Finally, Chap said, with a stammer, "I-I-I learned not to pee in-in the sandbox."

His father literally choked. Then his mouth tightened into a thin line, and his right eyebrow flew up. Leaping from his chair so quickly that it crashed over backwards, he grabbed Chap's arm and yelled, "My son will not be a low-class smart mouth!"

The soapsuds made Chap choke and sneeze and gag and cry all at the same time. Lori eventually rescued him by coaxing their father from the bathroom. Then she helped Chap rinse out the soap while trying to explain what had so infuriated their father. Through a blur of hurt and tears, Chap understood only that *pee* wasn't a nice word. It was years before he felt brave enough and defiant enough to say it again—and then not within earshot of Lori or his father.

The real lesson Chap learned at age five was that even if what he'd learned was not to pee in the sandbox—he'd heard Paulie Mason's sobs through the door of the principal's office—that was not necessarily what his father wanted to hear. Chap's habit of weighing words carefully before he spoke had begun.

By the time Chap was twelve or thirteen, their father had quit demanding a report every evening at the supper table. Sometimes he asked. Sometimes he didn't. Most often Lori volunteered news about her job at a computer company or maybe a movie she'd seen with a date, and occasionally Chap told about school, but their father appeared less and less interested. Eventually, the questioning had stopped completely. The pressure was off. Chap no longer rehearsed presentations with Lori while they fixed supper. The quieter meals suited Chap just fine since he preferred talking and laughing with Lori as they cooked and cleaned and did the laundry—and their father stayed behind the closed door of his den, writing about the history of war from the point of view of the common soldier.

* * *

That night as the meatloaf, cheese-creamed potatoes, and peas with sautéed mushrooms steamed on their plates, Lori said, "Dad, I have something to tell you and Chap. It's good news, really. I'm being promoted to assistant for Mr. Burris."

Their father looked up from his plate, his gray eyes on Lori, his fork suspended in mid-air.

"And I'm being transferred—just for a couple of months—to Alexandria to help him set up a training program there."

Their father's fork didn't move, but Chap dropped his.

"You're leaving?" he said more loudly than he intended.

And that was the big blip.

* * *

Chap didn't sleep much that night, flopping from side to side and stomach to back. Even the trees seemed restless, waving in the late summer wind. For hours, he thought of all the reasons Lori couldn't leave. She was a huge part of his predictable, stable life—the one who'd helped with homework when he was little, kept him on task around the house, and taken him to Riverwoods to purchase new jeans when his ankles started to show and new shoes when the old ones fell apart. She was the one who'd known how to put on the GI Joe band-aid without making the scrape hurt more and the one who'd enforced their father's rule of eating three bites of everything on the plate while pretending not to notice when Chap hid carrots in a napkin. She was the one who'd stayed home after all the others left, giving up a scholarship to Ball State and going, instead, to work for Mr.

Burris while taking night classes to get her associates from Wandering River Community College. She was the one who still did the parent-type stuff that his friends' mothers or fathers did for them—and the one who talked to him. He couldn't imagine life in the big house with one more empty bedroom down the hall.

Then as the gray light of dawn broke over the high trees and crept into the room, Chap toyed with the idea of change, trying to envision freedom from the only pair of eyes that paid much attention to him. Not that Lori was bossy, even for a big sister. But if she were hundreds of miles away and their father stayed holed up in his den, hour after hour, day after day, Chap could quietly skip some of the inside chores she delegated, watch television or read as late as he pleased, and mow the yard less often. With that thought, he finally slept.

* * *

The next morning Chap stumbled down the back stairway to the kitchen, bleary-eyed from lack of sleep. But there would be no rest for the weary. Lori was already scurrying from room to room, packing her clothes and gathering all sorts of other stuff even though the little apartment that had been rented for her in Alexandria was furnished. No sooner had Chap finished a bowl of cereal than she shoved a tablet into his hands and began dictating endless instructions about what he should do about this and that. There was the check for school registration under the lighthouse magnet on the refrigerator and the number of the furnace man to call in September for the annual maintenance check and the gauge to watch on the LP tank. Chap flipped to another page of the yellow pad as she talked. Then Lori taped a list of everything he knew how to cook on the inside door of a cupboard and dictated a long grocery list of the ingredients needed since their father no longer drove to Riverwoods every Thursday to shop as he once had.

When Chap was little, he'd hop off the bus and run as fast as he could up the lane on Thursdays because Thursday was Reward Day. His father would gaze at him in mock seriousness and say something like, "I think my son knows how to multiply by six," and Chap would rattle off, "Six times one is six, six times two is twelve, six times three is eighteen, six times four is twenty-four . . ." until his father would pull a surprise out of a sack on the middle of the oak table. His father thought of endless ways to test Chap—how fast could he run up the lane, how well could he make his bed military style, or how quickly could he find words in the big red dictionary in the living room. The surprises were as varied, like a book from the library or a gallon of vanilla ice cream with a pint of big, juicy strawberries or a can of mixed nuts or a new deck of Uno cards—a game the Smith family played often with cutthroat enthusiasm.

It seemed odd that Chap couldn't remember when Reward Day began to happen less and less often and eventually stopped altogether even though the Thursday shopping trips continued—at least until the past year or so when his father would sometimes forget. Then Chap and Lori, her mouth all tight and her eyes tired, would drive to Krogers in Riverwoods after supper for groceries and cash for the week from an ATM.

* * *

The last Thursday Lori was home, all three of them went to Riverwoods to get school supplies, hair cuts, and a huge cartful of groceries.

On Friday there was no escape to read at the Church Rock because Lori decided to thoroughly clean the downstairs and catch up on the laundry. Between vacuuming rooms, Chap ran up and down the stairs to the basement, hauling load after load of sheets, towels, and clothes—five loads to be exact. As he peeled potatoes for supper, he again toyed with the idea that change might not be so bad.

But early the next afternoon, as Lori stood by her l
gray Honda, which was so stuffed she'd had to tuck
pairs of shoes into tiny spaces after discarding th
Chap had second thoughts. She was really leaving
thudded painfully.

On the front porch nearby, their father stood with his arms limp at his sides, dressed, despite the August heat, in jeans, a worn gray sweatshirt beneath an old khaki shirt frayed at the collar, and shoes with the laces untied. He'd said nothing to Lori when she hugged him—no last-minute route suggestions, no last-minute instructions. Even though Chap had gotten used to his father's quiet ways, the total silence was unexpected.

By the car, Lori hugged Chap. Then with her hands on his shoulders, she stepped back a bit to look at him, reading his thoughts as she often did. "You'll do fine, Chap," she said. "I'll be back before you have a chance to neglect taking care of this place."

She smiled—Chap didn't smile back—then hugged him again, blew a kiss to their father, and slid behind the wheel of the car. In seconds, it disappeared, leaving only a faint cloud of dust hanging over the lane.

Chap turned around. His father stood as before, staring at the place where the car had last been visible. "I'm alone," he said.

"I'm here," Chap said.

Moving towards the front door, his father said again, "I'm alone."

When the door to the den slammed shut, Chap said loud to no one, "You're not the only one who's alone."

* * *

Within a week after Lori left, Chap knew that any thought he'd had about change being good was wrong, dead wrong. Life alone with his father was neither free nor fun. And going back to school didn't help. There was a lot to do, and he missed Lori. She was his best friend—at least in secret. Disliking sisters was the norm with the guys around the cafeteria table, and going beyond tolerating a sister to liking one would really cause the eyebrows to shoot up. Because Chap managed to inspire that kind of reaction from his friend Tom and the guys often enough anyway, he decided not to tell anyone that Lori was gone. They'd never understand why that wasn't good news.

Soon one monotonous day was blending into another as Chap jogged to and from the bus stop, attended classes, and did homework with varying degrees of enthusiasm. He also cooked, cleaned, and did the laundry, all without Lori's chatter and the laughter that had made living in the big house in the woods eight miles from town pleasant.

The door to the den was closed most of the time Chap was home, opening when his father came out for supper. His father spoke little, and Chap could barely remember the last time his father had smiled. After Lori called home the first time, his father said again, as he left the kitchen, "I'm alone."

Chap held his tongue until he heard the door to the den close. Then banging the dirty pans around in the sink, he said, loudly enough to feel better but not loudly enough for his father to hear, "You can go to hell!"

Chapter 2

The only disturbance of the thud-thud, thud-thud of Chap's boring routine during the first month after Lori left was when a new girl criticized his paper in English class, and that never would've happened if a couple of weeks earlier Mrs. Hunt hadn't announced that the students were to write an autobiography for their first major paper. Such an assignment was no surprise to those who'd survived her ninth grade English class since she had a well-deserved reputation as a real taskmaster when it came to composition. Most had rewritten at least one paper before figuring out that it was easier to do it right the first time than to try to sneak "garbage" past her poised red pen—"garbage" being what she called anything less than her students' best work.

Even so, English was Chap's favorite class and Mrs. Hunt his favorite teacher—not that he shared that information with anyone, especially not Tom, who had very definite ideas about what a guy should and shouldn't like. English and English teachers definitely fell into the latter category.

After Mrs. Hunt gave the assignment, Tom wrinkled up his freckled nose as they were leaving class and declared in his no-one-can-possibly-disagree-with-me style, "There's no way that busybody's going to learn anything personal about me!"

Chap hesitated, trying to figure out how Tom intended to write an impersonal autobiography. He almost said, "That's an oxymoron," but he might've had to explain that, and his rumbling stomach urged him towards lunch. Instead, he said, "Mrs. Hunt's not so bad."

Tom rolled his gray-green eyes and said, "Right, Chap," in a tone implying that even Chap surely couldn't believe the words that had tumbled from his mouth.

Sometimes Chap wondered why he bothered to talk to Tom at all since they disagreed a lot more often than not. Actually, there was no reason to expect the friendship to be too agreeable. After all, there had been a problem the very first time they'd laid eyes on each other four years earlier. Tom had been a real pain in the butt even then.

That day a bunch of sixth-grade guys were playing basketball during outdoor recess like usual when this shrimpy new kid, wearing a wild Hawaiian blue and white print shirt and a smirky smile, snatched the ball and ran with it. The guys screamed and yelled and threatened his life, but he just taunted them, darting in and around all the other kids on the playground and demanding that the guys race him to get the ball back. Yeah, like they were going to do that.

But everyone failed to catch him.

The girls, having stopped their activities to watch, began to snicker. That narrowed the options in a hurry. Reluctantly, the guys agreed to race the little twerp a few at a time. That would shut him up—and the girls, too.

Wrong.

He didn't look like much of a runner, being so short and scrawny, but he was fast, real fast, and he was winning every heat even while holding onto the basketball.

Chap was in the last group. By that time, the kid was looking irritatingly smug, and Chap was feeling just plain irritated. At "Go," Chap burst forward with all his might, ahead right from the start. When Chap led by a full stride, the kid heaved the basketball at Chap's legs. Chap smashed onto the concrete sidewalk, hands down, scraping the skin off both palms and doing real damage to his jeans. Without saying a word, he sprang up, doubled up his stinging hands, and slugged the kid in the nose.

When Mr. Walker, the playground supervisor, got to them, they were standing not quite chest to chest—Chap was several inches taller—dripping blood and glaring silently at each other.

"Who started it?" Mr. Walker demanded, grabbing their collars and jerking them apart.

"It wasn't a fight," the kid said loudly. "It was an accident."

Frowning, Mr. Walker looked at Chap, who looked down at his bloody hands.

"An accident. Honest," the kid said, wide-eyed and innocent-looking. "Our feet got tangled up in a race."

"No fight, huh?" said Mr. Walker.

"No, sir, no fight. We know better than to fight, don't we?" the kid said, giving Chap a friendly-looking but solid punch on the arm.

Chap nodded without looking up.

"All right," Mr. Walker said as he pulled his reading glasses down from the top of his closely cropped gray hair and scrawled "fell on the playground" across the accident report sheet he carried around with him on a green clipboard. "Now let's get you two cleaned up."

Together they went to the nurse's office where Chap got the soap-peroxide-gauze treatment while the kid sat with his head back and a cold cloth on his bloody nose.

The next day the kid shoved a shopping bag into Chap's lap as he sat at his desk. "Size 14 slims," he said quietly, his eyes down. "My mom said to bring 'em back if they don't fit."

After glancing into the bag at the new jeans, Chap stammered not "Thank you," as he'd been taught, but "Your nose isn't so swollen today."

Grinning, as he punched Chap's arm, the kid said, "Hey, my name is Tom—Thomas Tom Thompson, to be exact."

"For real?" Chap said, grinning right back.

"Yeah, for real, but I don't suppose you're going to have too much smart to say about it since I hear your name is Chap."

Somehow with that new pair of jeans and a pair of weird names, they became a duo at school even though they turned out to be a lot more different than alike.

Chap grew taller with dark wavy hair and pale skin. Tom stayed short with curly sandy hair and a million freckles. He liked to talk and blurted out whatever popped into his mind. Chap was more cautious. He needed to think about the words first. Often the opportunity to speak was gone before he'd decided what to say.

Maybe that explained what Chap liked about writing. He had total control with time to think and plan and change the words if he didn't like what he'd written. But once he opened his mouth, the words were out there, and he couldn't suck them back in and change them even if what he'd said made him sound like a jackass.

Chap liked the idea of writing an autobiography for Mrs. Hunt and, for some insane reason, said so as he and Tom joined the cafeteria line. Chap knew he'd made a mistake as soon as Tom rolled his eyes again, but there was no way to get those words back.

"You like to write!" Tom said in the same incredulous tone he would've used if Chap had confessed to wearing pink silk pajamas. "Real men don't like to write!"

Tom's "real men" cracks always irked Chap, especially since his father had been writing for years, so he snapped back, "Real men don't write? What about Hemingway?"

"Who?"

"Ernest Hemingway."

Tom's face showed zero recognition.

"Ernest Hemingway, novelist, story writer. He won both the Pulitzer Prize and the Nobel Prize."

Tom's face remained blank.

"*The Old Man and the Sea*—you know, the story we read last year in English," Chap said with increasing impatience.

"Oh, that Hemingway," Tom said, brightening.

"Gee," Chap said with a grimace, "there must be dozens of writers named Hemingway."

Ignoring the sarcasm, Tom said, "That was one dumb story. The old guy hooked a fish, fought it for most of the book, and then failed to land it. No one even saw it. What was the point?"

"My point is Hemingway was manly. He was a war correspondent, even got wounded. He hunted, fished, and loved women. He wrote manly stuff."

"Okay. He's one example. What about all the other writers?"

Years of experience had taught Chap when to shut up, and that moment was an excellent time to do so since the conversation was going nowhere.

"Ah, forget it," Chap said. "What's for lunch?"

Without mentioning the assignment again to Tom, Chap began the autobiography that night, writing and rewriting every evening until he finished it right before the due date.

* * *

About a week after turning in his autobiography, Chap was daydreaming during class, really gone. That was unusual since he liked English. Most often he had trouble concentrating in study hall or in algebra, which made about as much sense as Russian. But that day the tall, multi-paned windows were open. The breeze was very warm for September. The gray clouds building in the west beyond the ball fields prompted Chap to wonder if rain would give the tired grass the incentive to green up once more and make the chrysanthemums around the house burst into color or if it would bring cold and maybe frost. He imagined the woods as they would smell when the trees blazed in shades of scarlet, gold, rust, and bronze.

"Chap?"

He jumped.

"You're a long ways away," Mrs. Hunt said, her dark eyes peering intently over the top of her half glasses. "I think you may want to hear about these," she added, nodding towards a stack of papers on her desk.

"The good news is you're writing correctly more often than not," she said to the class. "Almost no technical errors. You write complete sentences and clear paragraphs. You know where commas go, and you've apparently looked up a lot of words. It's great to be starting the year with the majority of you writing standard English. However—"

"I hate the word *however*," Tom blurted out. "It always means bad news."

Several students laughed, but they stopped when Mrs. Hunt frowned.

"Sorry, Thomas," she said before continuing. "For the most part, your papers are boring, put-me-to-sleep boring. I seemed to be reading forms with the blanks filled in because the majority of you began with 'I was born'—fill in where and when. 'I have ___ brothers and ___ sisters. My parents are ___' or 'I live with ___.'"

She was pacing, talking with her hands. "You told about your life in chronological order. 'When I was one, I walked. When I was two, I talked. When I was five, I started kindergarten' and so on. I'd like to have a dollar for every sentence that started 'When I was.'"

A ripple of nervous laughter went around the room. Chap smiled even while remembering sentences like that in his paper.

"Some of you included details—things like a favorite grandparent, a camping trip, a hobby, a broken bone, or some special talent—but most of you failed to present yourselves as unique individuals. Feelings, attitudes, and reactions were glaringly absent. For example, 'Our house burned down when I was seven. I hit a homerun when I was eight.'"

Some students laughed again, including Chap. Mrs. Hunt often used exaggerated examples to illustrate writing problems. One day last year, she'd walked up to Ginger Estelle's desk, picked up her entire stack of books, and slammed them onto the floor with a resounding crash. Even those not half-asleep jumped. Then she walked back to her desk and calmly told everyone to turn in the homework assignment. It was dead quiet in the room except for the rustling of papers. Students kept peeking at Ginger, trying to figure out what perfect-5.0-average-since-sixth-grade Ginger could've done to upset Mrs. Hunt. After everyone turned in the homework—everyone except Ginger, who was apparently afraid to touch her stuff that was strewn about on the floor—the class started to analyze a short story.

Halfway through a discussion about the effects of the third person omniscient point-of-view, Joe Hardy jumped up, pointed at the mess on the floor, and said, "Why'd you do that to her books?"

"No reason," Mrs. Hunt said with a shrug.

Almost shouting, Joe said, "No reason? You had to have a reason!"

"Oh, so you expect people to have reasons and motives for what they do?"

"Sure," he said as others nodded.

"Well, then," she said, "why did so many of the characters in the short stories you wrote act without reasons? I read story after story where perfectly reasonable people suddenly, without any apparent motives, committed violent acts or inexplicably did insane things."

At that point, Ginger began to pick her stuff up off the floor, grinning smugly about her part in the lesson, which, it turned out, she and Mrs. Hunt had planned earlier that day. Those who'd felt sorry for Ginger immediately quashed their sympathy. She'd get no Oscar nomination from her classmates.

Mrs. Hunt had continued to explain how the students had failed to develop their characters adequately. She was making the same kind of point about the autobiographies. The students had failed to develop themselves.

"Without emotions or reactions," she said, "having your house burn down and hitting a homerun seem equally important. The individuality of the writer is hidden."

Dropping her hands, she picked up the top paper from the stack. "There are a few exceptional papers. I want to read you the beginning of one entitled 'Loss.'"

Chap's stomach flipped. That was the title of his paper. Nervously, he glanced at Tom and silently begged Mrs. Hunt not to tell the class who wrote it. With his heart pounding so hard he feared others could hear it and his blood racing around his body, he struggled to adopt a facial expression that showed a great lack of interest.

Mrs. Hunt began to read aloud.

> *I slow down as I approach the narrow wooden bridge that spans Wandering River. I am hoping to see the crane, who knows why, for it is an ungainly, ungraceful bird with legs too long and too spindly.*
>
> *I have been watching the crane since early last summer. One day as I sat on the bridge rail listening to the water gurgle over the rock piles below, the crane swooped over the trees, its wings widespread, its long legs stretched out behind, its neck folded in an s-curve. Never before had I seen such a bird close up. I began to walk from my house often to watch it. Sometimes the crane waded, slowly picking up one sticklike leg at a time. Sometimes it stood like a statue on a rock or a low willow branch, looking most regal with the long bluish-gray feathers on its head. Then when a minnow*

swam within reach, it plunged its head down lightning quick to spear the fish with its daggerlike beak.

Now I stop on the bridge and look carefully up and down the river, wondering if the crane has gone—gone to wherever cranes go when summer fades and the hint of early fall creeps into Indiana. I wonder if the crane has left me.

I am used to being left.

Mrs. Hunt stopped reading and slid the paper into the middle of the stack. She removed her glasses, letting them dangle from the chain around her neck. The room was silent. With his eyes glued on Mrs. Hunt, Chap concentrated on keeping his face frozen as he fought the conflicting emotions of fear of discovery by his classmates and unbounded joy from Mrs. Hunt's approval.

"That paper," she began, "didn't put me to sleep. I was interested right from the beginning. What did the crane have to do with the student's life?"

"Are you going to read the rest of it?" a guy asked.

"No, that would be an invasion of privacy. I considered not reading even this much, but the paper is an excellent example of a personal approach to the assignment. The unifying thread that runs throughout the autobiography is loss, and for this student, the crane symbolizes loss. Any questions or comments?"

A girl sitting up front raised her hand. She'd entered class a few days before. Chap stared at the thick dark braid that hung against her pale blue sweater. Having barely glanced at her before, he tried to picture her face but couldn't.

"There's a problem with the paper," she said.

Chap's stomach lurched.

"Oh? And what is that?" Mrs. Hunt said.

"The bird isn't a crane. It must be a heron, probably the great blue heron."

Chap's face was burning.

"How do you know?" Mrs. Hunt asked, her eyebrows raised.

"It's the neck. Herons fly with their necks in the s-shape. Cranes fly with their necks fully extended—"

The sharp clang of the bell and the immediate scraping of chairs cut her off. Above the din, Mrs. Hunt yelled, "No assignment. I'll return your papers tomorrow."

Chap exhaled to keep from exploding. With deep resentment at having his brief moment of recognition marred—no matter that it had been anonymous—he watched the girl pick up her books one at a time.

So how'd you get so smart? he challenged silently.

Finally, she stood and headed for the door, walking with a pronounced limp that favored her right leg. Chap felt better in a perverse sort of way. He might not know the difference between a crane and a heron, assuming she did, but at least he wasn't crippled.

* * *

Last hour Chap settled into his study hall seat and got out his algebra book. Ten minutes and only three problems later, he laid down his pencil.

"It must be a heron," the girl had said.

Crane? Heron? What's the big deal? he thought.

Apparently, Mrs. Hunt didn't know the difference between them either. Chap liked Mrs. Hunt, especially her journal writing assignments. He wasn't much good at participating in class, but they "talked" back and forth in his journal. The fact that her knowledge of large, gangly wading birds was also deficient made him feel a bit better.

Picking up his pencil again, he began to factor the third problem: $a^2 - 10a - 24$. He tried –8 and +3, then +8 and –3, followed by –6 and +4, +6 and –4. Nothing was working. Frustrated, he scratched out the whole problem and flipped the algebra book closed. Walking to the bulletin board, he got one of the library passes pinned there and signed out.

The library was almost empty, guarded by the formidable librarian, Mrs. Armstrong-Moore, whose curly fiery-red hair bounced around her face as she moved her head from side to side to keep track of those who might misbehave in her library. Tom and most of the other guys Chap knew avoided the library until having absolutely no other alternative except to go there, but Chap liked the library, even with Mrs. Armstrong-Moore watching his every move.

Taking an *H* encyclopedia to a table at the far end of the library, Chap read that the heron is a tall gaunt wading bird found on mud banks. It has an elongated neck, legs, and bill. Herons resemble cranes.

"Yeah, right," he mumbled.

According to the article, the eight-inch bill of the great blue heron is sharp-edged and pointed. There are four long-clawed toes on each foot, three directed forward and one backward. The middle front toe has a comb-like part used for preening the soft plumage. The heron has a feathered headdress. It stands about four feet tall and has a wingspan of six feet. It flies with its neck bent in an s-shape.

Slamming the book closed, Chap shoved back his chair, immediately attracting the attention of Mrs. Armstrong-Moore, who had hearing worthy of a mouse-pursuing cat along with her eagle eyes. She shushed him. Quietly, he replaced the encyclopedia between G and I, knowing that she was watching, and found the call number for a large pictorial bird book by John James Audubon. Chap copied the description of the great blue heron.

He has taken a silent step, and with great care he advances; slowly does he raise his head from his shoulders, and now, what a sudden start! His

> *formidable bill has transfixed a perch, which he beats to death on the ground. See with what difficulty he gulps it down his capacious throat!*

After reading some more and studying the bird in the picture, Chap checked the Dewey decimal number and returned the book to the right spot on the shelf. Before Chap was even out of the library, Mrs. Armstrong-Moore headed towards that area to be sure her precious book had been shelved correctly.

The dismissal bell was ringing when he re-entered study hall.

As Chap walked towards his locker, he saw Mrs. Hunt standing outside her room.

At first he considered pretending not to see her, but she smiled before he could look away.

"I looked it up," he said to her.

"I thought you might."

"The bird I saw is a heron. And you know what else? It could be migrating to the northern part of South America right now."

"See you tomorrow," she said, still smiling.

Chapter 3

In English class the next day, Chap was careful to keep his eyes away from the window. He concentrated on the daily usage drill and then began reading the assignment about methods used to develop a comparison and contrast paper. He was almost finished when Mrs. Hunt said, "I want to return your autobiographies before the bell rings."

Turning to the new girl, she said, "Will you finish what you were saying to the class yesterday about the bird?"

Heart thudding, Chap stared hard at the girl's back with the long braid in sharp contrast to the white sweatshirt she wore, willing her to feel uncomfortable.

"Oh, I already said it. Cranes fly with their necks extended and herons don't. That's all. It sounds like an interesting paper. I didn't mean to criticize," she said in a tone that sounded confident and not the least bit uncomfortable.

"Criticism, both positive and negative, is valuable to a writer. Don't apologize," Mrs. Hunt said, expressing an attitude about criticism not shared by Chap.

As she picked up the papers from her desk and began to pass them out, she continued, "Students, your assignment is to write a response to my criticisms of your paper." She paused until the groans died down. "That includes, of course, correcting errors by rewriting sentences or if necessary whole paragraphs, but more important, react to what I've said about your paper as a whole, especially if yours is one of the boring ones. Explain how you might present yourself as an individual. Be thoughtful. Make me believe I read your papers for some reason besides my desire to have no social life."

A girl sitting on the far side asked, "Will this help our grades?"

"I should think so," Mrs. Hunt said as she handed Chap his paper, "since you have no grades yet. You won't have until I see your responses."

More groans came from around the room.

"That's blackmail," Tom said loudly. "You're holding our grades for ransom."

"Right," she said with a laugh as the bell rang. "You've got two days to return with your autobiographies and ransom sheets in hand."

Quickly, Chap folded his paper and slid it into his back pocket so that Tom, who was waiting in the hallway, shifting impatiently from one foot to the other, wouldn't see the title.

"Get a move on," Tom demanded as Chap walked out of the classroom. "We're late for lunch."

As Chap tossed his books into his locker, Tom waved his red-splotched autobiography in front of Chap's face. "Can you believe this?" he said. "She wrote more on the paper than I did."

Then Tom maneuvered across the crowded hallway to his own locker, jerked open the unlocked door, pitched in his stuff, and slammed the door extra hard.

"It's just like old Mrs. Hunt to like a tear-jerk paper about some bird," he said, rejoining Chap. "It was written by a girl, no doubt, probably an orphan or one of those foster kids. No guy would care about some dumb bird you can't even hunt."

As they wove through the jostling crowd towards the cafeteria, Chap smiled. Tom had no clue that the paper was his.

After getting pizza slices and milk from the fast food line, they sat down with the usual bunch at a table in the center of the cafeteria. Between bites, Chap discreetly scanned the room, finally spying her long braid. She was sitting in the corner with two girls. One was tiny blond Mitzi somebody. The other one he didn't recognize at all.

When most of the guys at the table got into a big disagreement about how bad the Riverwoods High football team would whip the Panthers' butts on Friday, Chap nudged Tom and asked, "Do you know anything about that new girl?"

"What girl? Where?" Tom said, looking around.

"The girl in English class, the one who came last week," Chap said, trying to sound matter-of-fact.

"Oh, you mean the bird expert. She's hardly a looker with that scar."

"What scar?"

"You haven't seen her face?"

Chap shrugged. He'd seen only her back.

"You're slipping, good buddy, not checking out a new face even if she is a gimp," Tom said with a grin.

Chap winced, at least inside. He might think a word like *gimp*, but he'd never say it aloud, especially since Lori would kill him if she heard it. She hated words like that.

"Guess I've been preoccupied," Chap said.

"Lori on your case again?"

Tom thought Lori was too strict. Sometimes he said, "She's not your mother, you know," as if Chap needed to be reminded of that.

"No, she's not on my case." Chap hesitated then added, "Actually, she's in Virginia for awhile."

"You're home with just your father. Lucky you!" Tom said, grinning and slapping him on the shoulder.

"Sure," Chap said without smiling.

Tom thought Chap's father was cool since he rarely interfered in Chap's life—*interfered* being Tom's word. Tom's father, on the other hand, was big on interfering. He'd checked Tom's homework all during grade school and junior high. He showed up for parent conferences with Tom's mother, attended school activities, and expected to meet Tom's friends, even in high school.

Chap's father did none of those things. But what Tom thought was freedom from interference felt like—Chap searched for the right word. Then thinking of the closed den door and the silence that followed him from room to room in the big house, Chap decided he needed a new one to represent a little bit of neglect, a lot of loneliness, a smidgen of feeling unloved, and a hefty portion of being overworked. There would not be even a tiny fraction of feeling lucky in that word.

* * *

In last period study hall, Chap pulled the autobiography out of his pocket, carefully covering the title with his hand. Mrs. Hunt had written nothing throughout the paper, only a note at the end.

Someone my age expects to have suffered loss, and I have, but it pains me to know that someone your age has experienced so much as well. The tone of your paper makes me believe there is more to tell. Spending time with the crane is a recent part of your life, yet you use the crane to represent the loss of your mother and sisters that happened years ago. Time does not take loss away, but it blunts the pain, and your pain seems fresh.

Chap, your paper is A quality. I will not require a response from you, but if you want to "talk" in your journal, I'm here.

Chap refolded the paper and put it back into his pocket. Staring out the window, he weighed his options. He could tell Mrs. Hunt the truth. The pain was fresh. Lori was gone, and he was lonely since his father came out of his den only to eat, speaking little even then. Or he could stretch the truth and write that he was fine, maybe hint that he and his father were enjoying the bachelor life. In either case, Chap knew he'd have trouble putting his feelings into words for Mrs. Hunt, even on paper. A third possibility was not turning in a response at all, but he might have to explain that to Tom.

Chap had made no decision by the time the school day ended.

* * *

Hopping off the bus that afternoon, Chap began to jog down First Woods Road, another geographic name supplied by early settlers to the first of three roads in the area boxed by the river west of town—the other two predictably named Second Woods Road and Third Woods Road. Chap was well on his way north before the sound of the bus faded as it continued west along the highway. The quiet of the woods with the trees that canopied over the narrow, winding road was a part of his daily routine but an enjoyable part. When the township commissioner had declared the wooden bridge over Wandering River unsafe for the school bus several years earlier, Chap had chosen to walk the mile and a half to and from the highway instead of riding the bus thirty more minutes as it took the long way around. Even on the coldest, snowiest days, the wooded hills offered some protection from the wind.

But that day, the breeze was warm for late September. The sun, peeking through scattered gray clouds, cast pale leafy shadows on the blacktop. Chap stopped briefly on the bridge even though he didn't expect to see the heron. Then he jogged on. Thick patches of shaggy-headed golden rod as tall as a man filled the open spaces among the trees with dots here and there of white boneset, deep purple ironweed, and gently waving yellow compass flowers towering over all.

Chap still remembered the names. The summer he was ten, his father had decided to teach him about plants. A couple of times a week, they'd ventured from the house, once the dew had dried, with a knapsack full of water bottles, snacks, the *Audubon Society Field Guide to North American Wildflowers,* a tree guide, sketch pads, and colored pencils. For hours they walked, stopping often to thumb through the colored pictures of flowers to identify a plant. Sometimes they sat to sketch a tree or trace a leaf. By summer's end—the one they called the "botany summer"—Chap knew terms such as *lanceolate, basal, lobed, succulent*, and *bristle-toothed* related to leaves and *ray, spike, cluster, corolla*, and *sepal* related to flowers, and he could identify every wildflower his father pointed to with his walking stick.

The last day before school started that fall, they'd decided to see which wildflower was the tallest. Before leaving the house, his father marked heavy black lines at one foot intervals on his walking stick. Using his height of six feet plus the stick held straight up on top of his head, they found the giant to be a compass flower that was a smidgen over ten feet with ironweed coming in second at seven.

Although his father was not a man who smiled easily even then, Chap knew when he was pleased. He'd nod, and his face would relax, losing its military tenseness. That whole summer made a warm memory because his father had nodded often, and his eyes had smiled even if his mouth didn't.

Too bad, Chap thought as he jogged, there hadn't been a summer of—what was the *-logy* word for the study of birds? Slowing to a walk, he started through the alphabet to help him recall the word, the way his father had taught him: *A-logy, astrology, archeology, anthropology, B-logy, bryology, biology, C-logy, cosmology, cytology, chronology, choreology* . . . . The words were coming to mind quickly.

Chap had enjoyed the last project Mrs. Hunt had assigned in ninth grade English, the one Tom had complained about even more loudly than usual although he'd been Chap's partner and had let Chap do the lion's share of the work. After the class had read a lot of Greek myths, the students had paired off to create dictionaries of current words based on Greek and Roman word parts. Chap had been intrigued with the combinations, like *tele+graph = writing from a distance, tele+ phone = sound from a distance, tele + vision = sight from a distance* and *aqua + naut = sailor in water, astro+ naut = sailor to the stars* or the Russian version, *cosmonaut.* Their *-logy* list had been long.

Chap began to jog again, thinking of and rejecting *entomology, etymology, ethnology, geology, graphology, herpetology, hematology, hydrology, ichthyology, immunology, kinesiology, limnology, morphology, meteorology, neurology, ophthalmology*. He stopped in front of the mailbox, reaching inside to retrieve the newspaper and a couple of envelopes. With a smile, he thought of *oology*, which he thought both sounded funny and looked funny for a word which meant something as simple as the study of bird eggs.

Suddenly, the word was there— *ornithology*, the study of birds. That was what he'd needed, a course in ornithology. Maybe then he'd have learned the difference between a heron and a crane before making a mistake in a paper.

As Chap turned into the lane, the sun slid behind a cloud, stealing the pleasant memory of the botany summer and intensifying his gloomy thoughts about his flawed paper. The big white house appeared gray and forlorn. The upstairs shades were pulled down in the empty bedrooms, turning the windows into unseeing white eyes. The swing at the end of the porch that extended across the front of the house barely moved in the late afternoon breeze, and the red geraniums in flower pots flanking the three steps were withered and pale.

The place was too empty and too silent with Lori gone—not that their father had ever been a talkative man. In the past months, even before Lori left, he had spoken little. But that hadn't seemed to matter much when she was home because she was Chap's opposite—comfortable with words and quick to laugh. There were no long, empty silences when Lori was there.

Reaching the back of the house, Chap shifted his backpack, straightened his shoulders, and took a deep breath, feeling as if he were tackling a challenging stretch of mountain trail instead of four worn wooden steps to the back porch. Opening the door into the large kitchen, he yelled, "I'm home," even though he'd long since quit expecting to hear a response.

Chap didn't smell the smoke until he dropped his backpack and the mail onto the round oak table. It wasn't the faint smell of his father's pipe that lingered in the rooms after he'd left them. It was real smoke.

Quickly, Chap patted the dirty pans on the stove and checked the trash basket. Nothing. He returned to the back porch and sniffed, but the outside air was fresh. He dashed back into the kitchen—stomach churning, heart pounding. The smell was inside the house. Moving quickly, he touched all the pans again, the microwave and the toaster oven, too, and stuck his arm into the oven. All were cool. Crossing the kitchen, he sniffed everywhere. The odor was strong in the dining room and stronger yet in the living room. His eyes were smarting.

As he rushed across the front hallway to the closed door of the den, his eyes began to tear, yet he hesitated before knocking, ever fearful of disturbing his father as he worked.

Heart pounding, Chap knocked once, more loudly the second time.

"Sir, I smell smoke!"

No answer.

He turned the knob and pushed open the door. His father was sitting in the chair behind his desk, staring at the smoke rolling from the wastebasket.

"Fire!" Chap yelled.

His father looked at him with his right eyebrow raised and a puzzled expression on his pale face.

"Some . . . someone," he said.

Before Chap could move, a tongue of flame shot up dangerously close to some newspaper pages hanging over the edge of the desk. Chap dashed into the room and grabbed the metal wastebasket.

"Damn!" he yelled, dropping it and shaking both hands.

His father didn't move. Chap snatched up thick newspaper sections lying on a chair nearby and gingerly picked up the basket again. The orange-yellow flames were eating the crumpled paper inside. Backing quickly out of the den, he raced to the front door, set the basket down, and fumbled with the lock. Then he dashed down the front steps. Eyes burning, he flung the basket onto the grass and kicked it over. As the flames died down, Chap saw, among the glowing bits of paper and ashes, his father's blackened pipe.

Anger flooded every part of Chap's body, replacing the fear. Fists clenched and jaws tight, he backed away from the smoking ashes, turned, and raced down the lane then south along First Woods Road, not jogging but running full out.

His feet smacking the asphalt drowned out the pounding of his heart. Soon he had to slow down to a walk. His cheeks burned, his lungs ached. He gasped for breath as if still surrounded by the smoke.

Reaching the bridge, Chap scrambled down to the grassy bank of Wandering River. Dropping to his knees, he pounded the ground with his fists.

"You stupid son of a bitch!" he screamed. "You could've burned down the house! Stop with the games!"

He dropped flat onto his stomach—his arms and legs spread-eagled, his face buried in the grass—and sobbed.

* * *

It seemed like a long time until Chap could breathe normally. He raised himself first to his knees. Then when his legs weren't too wobbly, he stood up. A school of minnows swam lazily in the shallows. The weeks of warm, dry weather had caused Wandering River to shrink to a small creek, hardly worthy of being called a river. Small isolated pools were covered with thick green algae, and there was no longer any gurgling sound as the water barely moved among the rocks. Though it was as serene as ever in the waning light, the peace Chap had found there during the summer was gone. His stomach hurt.

His father's games. It seemed that he'd had Chap in training since birth. His father might not show up at school or demand to meet Chap's friends, but his father definitely interfered in his life, contrary to what Tom believed. Their home had been as regimented as any military post with regularly scheduled meals, weekly room inspections, and daily recitations. And for Chap, his only son, he had created what he called "games" to test his physical and mental abilities. Chap never knew when he would be confronted with some problem to solve. But this game of how to keep the damn house from burning down had a new twist—it was dangerous and stupid!

With eyes closed, Chap whispered, "Lori, please come home soon. Please come soon."

Since she was away from home only temporarily, Chap hadn't mentioned her absence in his autobiography. His father had shown no interest in the paper—only shrugging his shoulders and saying, "Later," when Chap had asked about his grandparents and his childhood. When "later" was obviously not going to come before the paper's due date, Chap asked Lori for help during one of her regular phone calls home. Being eight years older, she remembered what it was like when he was little. Besides that, she had their mother's diary.

Sitting down beneath a gigantic cottonwood tree with branches that stretched out over the water, Chap thought of the losses he'd written about, the ones Mrs. Hunt knew were too personal to share with the class. He took the folded paper from his pocket and turned to the second page.

I am used to being left. When I was not quite three, my mother left. Actually, she died. She was gone before I had a chance to know her, and I think I would have liked her—the pretty lady with the large gentle eyes who gazes at me from the pictures in the attic.

When I was six, my oldest sister, Catherine Adele, eloped with John, her high school sweetheart, and headed to Oregon. She has never come back, not even to introduce us to her daughter. I didn't get to know her very well either.

The next year it was Julianna Marie, sister number two. She went to college to become a painter but ended up in Kansas City designing greeting cards. She was home for three days a year ago Christmas.

Six months after Julianna left, Marilee Bethany—she was seventeen—packed an overnight bag, stole about five hundred dollars from the secret drawer in our father's desk, and caught a bus to Hollywood. He was so furious I hid in the attic for days. Marilee has never been back either, but every once in awhile we get a postcard from her. She still thinks she'll get a big break and make it in the movies. My sister Lori says she'd best keep her day job. I think I know what that means.

That left only three of us in the big, five-bedroom, two-story white house in the woods at the base of a hill:

Charles Henry, my father, a retired military man; Loretta Elizabeth, who was fifteen, and seven-year-old me.

Lori says my father wanted a son each time my mother was pregnant, a son to carry on his name and his military career. Only his son—that's me—would go to college and be an officer like he'd wanted to be, but depression and bottles of whiskey hidden in the rafters of the tumbledown barn had beat his own father until one rainy night he blew his brains out in the woods. He left his widow, who had no backbone and fewer skills, to raise their son—my father—alone. My father's dreams of West Point had slipped away into cheerlessness and poverty. He dropped out of high school midway through his junior year, forged his mother's signature, and joined the army. He returned to the shabby house of his youth only once—to bury his mother beside his father.

Then came duty overseas and several more years of service States side before he met my mother, Mary Jane White, at a USO dance. He courted her properly on Sunday afternoons before marrying her in her parents' living room.

As they trekked from military base to military base, the babies came with precision, one every other fall for eight years—all girls. Father named each one. Lori says he believes that if people have a common last name like Smith, they need distinctive first names, and he tolerated no nicknames except Lori's and mine (but the story of my naming comes later). Catherine Adele was never Cathy, nor was Julianna Marie ever Julie, nor Marilee Bethany either Mary or Beth. Only Loretta Elizabeth got to be Lori because she has always been his favorite.

I was born when my father was forty-five, already retired from the military, and my mother was thirty-eight. I believe I was an "accident," if you know what I mean. It was a difficult birth.

According to Lori, my father took my four sisters to the hospital when my mother got strong enough to hold me. They all stood around her bed. Only her dark hair seemed to separate her from the whiteness of the sheets. I was to be introduced. My father expected me to be named Charles Henry, Jr., of course. However, I was born on my mother's father's birthday, so she announced that my name would be Anthony Peter after her father.

My father got all tight-lipped and insisted so loudly that I be named Charles Henry that all my sisters cried. A nurse came in and demanded he speak quietly or leave immediately. That plus my mother's ashen face settled him down, and a compromise was reached. On the fifth day of my life, I got saddled with a name longer than my body: Charles Henry Anthony Peter Smith.

Thank heavens someone in the family knew about acronyms. I've been called Chap for as long as I can remember.

I was so little when my mother died that I hardly realized there was one less dark-haired, dark-eyed woman taking care of me. I was not neglected. One sister or another kept my clothes clean, my stomach filled, my room orderly, and later my lunch box packed. But when I was seven and a half, they were all gone—all except Lori and my father. I was old enough to miss my sisters as I miss the crane now.

It's a heron. I should have said heron, Chap thought as he refolded the paper. His stomach rumbled. On legs that felt stiff and sore, he climbed the bank and stood in the center of the road, not wanting to return to that house but having nowhere else to go. Finally, hands in his pockets, head down, he began to walk north as the sun slipped behind the wooded hills.

In the fading, grayish light, he cleaned out the wastebasket and carried both it and the badly charred pipe back to the den. The door was open.

"Sir, here's the wastebasket. I think your pipe is ruined."

Chap held the pipe out to his father, waiting for him to critique the performance, hoping to receive a bit of praise for keeping the fire contained. Chap wanted his father to acknowledge that he'd won the game.

The desk lamp, the only light in the room, made a bright circle, which encompassed his father and part of the huge cluttered desktop. His bristly gray hair matched the staring gray eyes. Suddenly, Chap realized how old he looked with his shoulders rounded, his pale skin sagging beneath his eyes, and the lines around his mouth deep creases. When his father didn't speak or reach for the pipe, Chap laid it on the desk.

"I'll fix us some supper now," Chap said barely above a whisper as he backed out of the den.

In the kitchen, he brushed some cracker crumbs from the table and rinsed out a glass that looked as if peanut butter had been smeared inside the rim. Then he took hamburger out of the refrigerator, found the other ingredients for sloppy joes, and got the covered skillet from the cupboard. Removing the lid, he startled. Inside the skillet lay a neatly folded pair of his father's black socks.

"Damn it!" he yelled towards the den. "I don't need more games. I've already got too much to handle with Lori gone."

Skillet in one hand and socks in the other, Chap waited for his father to answer. He didn't.

Finally, laying the socks on the table, Chap walked to the stove and started to brown the hamburger. There didn't seem to be anything else he could do.

Chapter 4

All of them were at the front door—all four of his dark-haired, dark-eyed sisters, dressed identically in jeans and pale blue sweaters—and he couldn't remember which one was which. Was that one Marilee? Or Catherine? Or Julianna? He couldn't even remember which one was Lori.

Mrs. Hunt began introducing them one at a time, but as Chap reached out to shake hands, each moved backwards across the porch and disappeared into the shadow of an enormous bird whose flapping wings darkened the front yard. Over and over, each sister approached the door with her hand extended. Though he struggled again and again to grasp the hands thrust towards him, their fingertips barely missed before each sister faded into the blackness and the confusion beyond the porch.

All the time, Mrs. Hunt was smiling and saying, "See. They are not lost. They are not lost."

Moments later, orange and blue flames started darting around Mrs. Hunt. Desperately, Chap tried to move, but his feet were cement-block heavy, and his arms hung uselessly.

Mrs. Hunt kept smiling and saying, "They are not lost," as the fire climbed higher and higher.

Chap fought the deadening weight of his body, shoving and pushing muscles that refused to move, but he was immobilized. When her silvery hair burst into flames, he bolted upright in bed, eyes wide. Gasping for breath, sweat and tears streaming down his cheeks, he stared into the darkness, forcing himself to inhale, exhale, inhale evenly.

Minutes later, when he could breathe normally, Chap got up and wandered throughout the house, upstairs and down, checking for smoke. Even after he knew there was no fire, he didn't sleep.

* * *

As streaks of lavender and rose crept into the grayish predawn sky, Chap struggled out of bed. A long hot shower didn't make him feel better, nor did a breakfast of milk, a banana, and raisin toast. Grabbing his backpack, he left the silent house.

The pastel shades in the early morning sky had given way to deep pink and orange that bounced off the clouds above. Many birds had already migrated, but several cardinals, which would stay the winter, were flitting from tree to tree, and the sparrows chirped tunelessly.

It was early yet. Instead of jogging to the bus stop, Chap wanted to walk, but even walking made his head throb. Ignoring the glorious sunrise, he looked down at the dark road to protect his burning eyes from the morning light. Stopping from habit at the bridge, he looked up and down the river for the heron despite knowing it was gone, the red-winged blackbirds and the kingfishers, too. Then he walked on towards the bus stop.

When a quick glance at his watch indicated that the bus wouldn't arrive for another fifteen minutes, Chap stepped off the left side of the blacktop and moved a few yards into the woods. Dropping his backpack beneath an old shagbark hickory tree, he sank down wearily. Within minutes, a young gray squirrel peeked over a branch, chattering its displeasure at the intrusion. Then it raced along the branch, leaped to a nearby oak, and scrambled down the trunk, stopping again to scold before disappearing.

The sound of a vehicle coming down First Woods Road broke the silence, a rarity so early in the morning. An old blue pick-up with one fender a deeper shade of blue rounded the last curve and stopped near the corner. Both doors opened. The driver, a man in a dark suit and tie, walked to the back of the truck and lifted out a bicycle.

"Are you sure you should do this yet? It's almost three miles," he said to the girl who came around the backside of the truck.

Sticking his head out just a bit from the back side of the hickory tree, Chap looked—then stared. She limped.

"I can do it. Actually, the doctor said I should," she said, laughing. "Let's hide the bike over here."

They pushed the bike to a clump of bushes close to the edge of the other side of the road. After the bike was concealed, they walked back to the truck. The man kissed her on the forehead, climbed into the truck, and drove off. The girl limped out to the highway and stood by the stop sign.

Chap stayed rooted to that spot behind the tree until the rumble of the bus could be heard in the distance. Two more squirrels had appeared, but he'd stared at the girl's back not them. As the bus rattled to a stop, he dashed from the woods, backpack in hand, and jumped on, pushing past the girl in the aisle and dropping into his usual seat in the back. Glaring at her dark braid, Chap wondered if the day could get any worse.

* * *

By not going to his locker, Chap successfully avoided Tom until fourth period English, their first class together.

Chap was almost to the room when Tom yelled, "Hey, Chap, wait up."

Chap stopped.

"Gee, man, you look awful," Tom said, grinning and punching his arm. "Didn't you sleep without Lori to tuck you in?"

"Leave it be," Chap said, trying to sound calm despite the tightness in his jaws.

"Oh, we're touchy today, aren't we?" Tom said, backing up with his hands raised in mock surrender.

"I said leave it be!"

The smile left Tom's face. "Sorry, but you really don't look too good."

Turning towards the classroom door to hide his face, Chap said, "I'm fine. I watched TV all evening then studied late."

"Bad idea, Chap."

Chap glanced at Tom, whom he often pictured with a frayed straw hat clamped on top of his sandy curls, a wheat straw dangling from his mouth, and a lopsided grin imprinted on his freckled face—a sort of modern Tom Sawyer look-alike. At that moment, however, the impish smile was gone, replaced by a serious expression, maybe even a concerned one. But before Chap had time to explore that rarely revealed side of his friend, the ornery grin returned as Tom punched him in the arm again. Chap was forever bruised.

"Here comes the bird girl," Tom said.

Before Chap could duck into the room, he saw her smile. Unfortunately, so did Tom, who rolled his eyes. At that point, Chap was absolutely positive the day was a disaster.

"What's the bit with her?" Tom said.

"What bit?"

"The smile, lover boy. Why the smile?"

"Oh, that. I guess it's because she rides my bus," Chap said in his most casual, unconcerned tone.

Tom stared a few moments. Then apparently satisfied with the explanation, he said with a shrug, "Probably," and walked into the room.

* * *

When the bus slowed down for First Woods Road that afternoon, Chap started down the aisle in order to be at the door before the girl stood up. He stepped off, slipped on his backpack, and began jogging north immediately. He didn't take time to stop at the bridge, but he heard the bike before getting much beyond it. She pulled along side, pedaling slowly to keep pace.

"You wrote the paper about the heron, didn't you?" she said.

Chap didn't speak.

"I saw it from the bridge," she continued, "when we came to look at our house."

Silence.

"Your paper was good, really."

Chap kept jogging, looking straight ahead but seeing her peripherally anyway. Her dark hair shone in the sun. She was tall and slender like he was. His heart was pounding, not only from running. He knew he should be saying something, but absolutely nothing came to mind.

She spoke again. "I'm supposed to ride my bike to make my leg muscles stronger. I've worn a brace most of this year and a cast most of last."

Silence.

"I got run down by a drunk driver."

"Too bad," he said without looking at her face.

Chap hadn't meant to be insincere, but as soon as those two little words hit his ears, he realized how sarcastic they sounded. Since there was no way to suck them back in and make them sound better, he jogged on in silence.

She stopped her bicycle.

"What's your problem anyway?" she yelled at his back.

Chap stopped running, but he didn't turn around. She walked her bicycle up and parked it sideways right in front of him. He looked at her face directly for the first time. Tom was right. The dark-red jagged scar, which started at the hairline by her left cheek and cut beneath her eye to the bridge of her nose, wasn't pretty. But her eyes were a beautiful deep-sea blue-green, and they were threatening to fill with tears.

"No problem," he said, dropping his gaze to the road. "I don't talk much to anyone."

"Got it," she said. "That excuses rudeness perfectly."

There was no doubt about her tone being sarcastic. With a flip of her braid, she mounted the bike and disappeared around the next curve.

* * *

The next morning the overcast sky muted the colors of the sunrise, allowing just a tinge of pink to show. A fast moving cold front had brought a brief but furious thunderstorm during the night, and it was much cooler. When Chap saw his breath in tiny puffs, he immediately regretted not having on his heavier jacket, but then he figured that being physically miserable made perfect sense since everything else in his life was such a mess. His father was acting weird; his sister was gone; his best friend treated him like a punching bag, and a know-it-all bird girl had invaded First Woods Road.

Chap kicked a rock from the edge of the blacktop, then another one harder, and another one before stopping to zip up his lightweight jacket. Then in a most sarcastic fashion, he chided himself for feeling ungrateful. After all, he thought, my father only *tried* to burn down the house—he didn't actually succeed.

Chap picked up a handful of stones and flung them one at a time through the shrubs along the road, listening to the sounds of the rustling leaves getting softer and softer as each stone sailed into the trees before dropping to the ground.

Besides not burning down the house, his father hadn't done anything else all week except eat the suppers Chap fixed. Twice Chap had tried to talk to him, first telling him it was getting colder and later telling him that he'd received an A on his English paper. His father had only stared, expressionless, as if a comment about the weather and news about a good grade were equally unimportant, neither one deserving a comment.

The hurt was in his stomach again. Chap hurled a final handful of stones into the underbrush, scaring the birds into silence, then looked at his watch. Only ten more minutes to bus time. He began to jog in order to get to the hickory tree before the girl got there—if she came at all.

Chap was only a few steps off the road when the truck rounded the bend in the road. From behind the closest big tree, he watched them remove the bike, hide it, and kiss just as they'd done the day before. When the bus arrived, he dashed from the woods, leaped on, pushed past her, and sat down just as he'd done before, too. And he'd managed to do all that without seeing her face and those eyes.

* * *

Waiting near their lockers, Tom said, without even a hello, "Was she on the bus?"

"Who?"

"You know who," he said with a frown and his mouth all crooked.

"Oh, you mean the bird girl."

"Yes, I mean the bird girl. Do I have to draw a picture?"

"She was on the bus. What's the interest?"

"No interest here," Tom said. "It's you she's after, lover boy."

"She is not after me. She doesn't even like me."

Immediately, Chap realized he'd said too much.

"So you have talked to her. When?" Tom said, smacking him on the back.

"We didn't talk," Chap said slowly, figuring that was close enough to the truth to meet Lori's tough criteria for honesty. The girl had talked, but he really hadn't said much. Surely, his few words couldn't count as real conversation. Chap's only other experience with a mouthful of soap had been at Lori's hands, and it'd convinced him that she was really narrow-minded about lying.

"So how do you know she doesn't like you?" Tom asked, peering at Chap suspiciously.

"I don't know for sure. I guess it's the way she looks at me," Chap said with a shrug.

Tom studied him like some biological specimen while Chap practiced his most nonchalant look. Tom apparently decided to buy that explanation.

"Oh, well," he said. "I thought you'd found your lady love."

"Didn't know I was even looking for one," Chap said, forcing a smile.

Locker doors up and down the hall were slammed as kids scurried towards their homerooms before the late bell rang.

"See you," Tom said.

"Later," Chap said.

* * *

In homeroom Chap hurriedly finished the response assignment for Mrs. Hunt, admitting that Lori was in Virginia for awhile and explaining that maybe he'd written about loss since he was living in a house without females for the first time in his life. Mrs. Hunt would understand that since she'd known all his older sisters in years past. Chap added that he and his father were surviving their bachelorhood.

Lori would say that Chap had committed the sin of omission since he'd left out some pertinent information.

He didn't include that he was doing all the work; he didn't describe his father's silence or the blank stares; he didn't confess that he was lonely in that big house, and he definitely didn't mention the fire.

All morning Chap dreaded going to English. Besides not being particularly happy with the response paper, he was anxious about a possible confrontation with the girl, but that worry turned out to be for nothing.

He was already seated when she came in. Before sitting down, she looked straight back, giving him a long look devoid of anger or belligerence or curiosity or amusement or dislike. Her eyes bored into him, but her face was empty of any expression he could identify. Chap hadn't known exactly what to expect, but he'd expected some reaction from her. She'd been angry—he'd imagined the tears spilling down her cheeks as she bicycled away. Last night while staring at the dancing tree shadows on the ceiling of his room, he'd tried to consider all the possibilities of what she might do. What he hadn't considered was the totally blank stare.

Chap tried to concentrate while the class finished a usage drill about objective case pronouns, but when he began to complete the exercises, his concentration failed completely. The girl's face with the intense blue-green eyes floated around the page.

The class was almost over before he suddenly realized why her stare was so upsetting. It was like the expressionless look on his father's face, the one that made Chap feel as low and unimportant as—after thinking about insignificant creatures, he finished the simile—a caterpillar.

* * *

Thus the deep-sea blue-green eyes became one more part of Chap's boring, miserable life. Thud-thud, thud-thud, thud-thud. He learned that her name was Erica Anderson. It'd been easy enough to read it upside-down on the seating chart when passing Mrs. Hunt's desk. Once in awhile he'd see Erica looking at him, but her face never changed, and she didn't speak. Every morning he stayed in the woods until the bus came. Every afternoon she biked past him a short distance beyond the wooden bridge.

At home his father still put his socks in odd places several times a week, but Chap no longer jumped back when they fell out of the freezer or showed up in a cereal bowl. His father hadn't yet given him a single clue about what this sock game was all about.

Besides that, his father had started a new one, equally mysterious. He was cutting paper napkins into four smaller squares, creating little caches in unexpected places like inside the unabridged dictionary, beneath a pot of violets that continued to thrive despite Lori's absence, and at the bottom of the dirty clothes hamper. Chap never saw his father with the scissors, but the little piles kept showing up.

For awhile Chap didn't refill the napkin holder, but when the little stacks continued to appear—made of toilet paper instead—he gave into the game and played his part, which was apparently to keep the napkin supply handy.

Worse than the games Chap didn't understand was the silence. Whole days passed when his father's conversation was a handful of single words—if any at all. Once his father's mouth had opened, but no sound had come forth. He raised his hands to his face, his fingers fluttering. Then pure anger flooded his face before he wheeled and fled to the den.

Meanwhile Chap's work schedule was fine-tuned. He was keeping the laundry done, the house cleaned, the dishes washed, and the meals fixed. His father's only contribution was the grocery shopping—at least it was supposed to be his contribution. Chap kept a list under the lighthouse magnet on the refrigerator door as Lori had always done. Sometimes the list was gone and the groceries were there when he got home on Thursdays. Sometimes they weren't. Several times when they were out of staples like bread and milk, they'd gone to Riverwoods together after Chap got home from school.

The only pleasant break in his miserable existence was when Lori called about once a week, "To check up on you," she said.

During one of their phone chats, she tried to take the credit for Chap's efficiency about the house—she was such a great example for him, she said—but he reminded her why he'd started doing the laundry on his own when he was twelve. She used to forget until none of them had a stitch of clean underwear. Lori had laughed, the laugh that Chap missed so much.

Chap had also told Lori about the A he'd received for his autobiography—the A his father had chosen to ignore. At least Lori was proud of him.

Then Chap said, "You know that big bird that stays near the wooden bridge—did you know it's a heron not a crane?"

"No. How'd you find that out?"

"Some girl mentioned it in front of the whole class when Mrs. Hunt read the first part of my paper aloud."

"Do I hear a problem with 'some girl'?" Lori said with a laugh.

Chap was silent.

"Oh, come on. You know I'm teasing. I didn't help raise some sort of chauvinist. What's she like?"

"She's a new girl, named Erica. They live farther north here."

Chap paused, almost ready to talk about the limp and the scar and the deep-sea, blue-green eyes that rarely looked at him. But he didn't.

"I don't really know her," he added.

"Maybe that'll change," Lori said before she said goodbye. Chap could "hear" the smile in her voice.

Each time Lori called home, he wasn't lonely, but then each call ended.

At school Tom decided the blank looks meant Erica really wasn't interested after all, so he talked about other interests like basketball and Suzy Barker, who was in his biology class and who wore teeny tiny skirts and equally skimpy tops, which made Tom very interested in the way she stood and bent over the table to dissect her frog. He spent the class first watching her from behind then going up front on one pretext or another to see the front view. When the dissecting unit was over, Chap was secretly gratified that Tom got a D- on the exam, figuring it served him right for paying so much attention to Suzy's anatomy and so little to the frog's.

The first quarter ended when the leaves were in full color. Chap got A's in all his classes except algebra. With an unsteady hand, he laid his report card on the table by his father's plate with the C- in full view and pointed to the line marked parent's signature. Surprisingly, his father signed without saying a word.

Chap wondered if Lori would be that easy when she came home.

Chapter 5

Tom's two great talents were running and math. Coach Rostek had discovered in p.e. class that Tom could run and dart while dribbling a basketball as well as he'd run and darted while holding onto one that first day in sixth grade. Even though Tom hadn't gone out for the basketball team as a freshman, the coach had made him a starting guard on the junior-varsity team as a sophomore.

Tom's interest in Suzy Barker had waned when the dissection unit ended and the colder weather caused her to break out her winter wardrobe of jeans and oversized sweaters and shirts. His desire shifted to Heather Landers, a junior cheerleader, who wore about the same amount of clothing when she didn't cheer as when she did. The tiny part of his attention not focused on basketball and Heather he gave to Chap, who was in desperate need of help with Algebra I.

Words had always made sense to Chap but not numbers. Tom, on the other hand, sneered at writers and read as little as possible, but he'd aced every math class he'd ever taken without breaking a sweat, even high school level algebra in eighth grade.

It'd taken Chap a week to build up enough courage to ask Tom for help. When he finally called, Tom said, "Sure, any time," as if Chap made such a request every day.

Tom turned out to be a patient, uncritical tutor, who managed to keep his mouth shut at their lunch table about Chap's way-lower-than-Lori-would-likely-accept math grade.

The frequent calls to Tom were the only variation in Chap's humdrum, boring life as October faded into November. Thud-thud, thud-thud. Mostly Tom and Chap talked about math with some diversionary details about Heather tossed in even though she seemed oblivious to Tom's adoration. Tom walked Chap through problem after problem, and it was helping. Chap got a B+ on the first chapter test that quarter and one C and one B on the quizzes for the next.

* * *

The first Thursday afternoon in November, Chap was staring out the window of the bus as usual. Only the most stubborn leaves still clung to the tree branches, waiting for the first winter storm to tear them off. The ground beneath the trees was carpeted in a thick layer of crisp tan leaves not yet damp and brown. The sun shone brightly, but there had been another killing frost the night before, and he'd dug out his heavy winter coat and lined gloves.

About a quarter of a mile from First Woods Road, the bus roared past a seemingly empty car parked at an odd angle with its front end tilted towards the deep drainage ditch that ran parallel with the highway.

"Stop the bus, Tony," Chap yelled, grabbing his backpack. "That's my father's car."

By the time Tony got the bus to a safe stop on the shoulder, the car was out of sight around the last curve.

"You going to need any help?" Tony asked.

"No, I'll just check out the car and then go on home. Thanks anyway," Chap said over his shoulder as he dashed down the steps.

The bus moved on towards First Woods Road, and Chap headed the opposite way towards the car. Running hard, he fought against the picture of his father sprawled across the car seat, unconscious and bleeding, with a mortally wounded deer lying nearby in the ditch.

Rounding the curve, he stopped. Then taking a deep breath, he cautiously approached the car, fearing that first look inside. But his father wasn't there, nor was there any sign of blood or a deer, just three sacks of groceries tilted at odd angles in the backseat. Feeling relief, Chap exhaled as he examined the car's exterior, which appeared undamaged. Even so, the car had come dangerously close to going over the side of the ditch, a drop of eight to ten feet.

Feeling a bit like an investigating state trooper, Chap walked further back to look for skid marks, but he found none. His initial relief was gradually being replaced with uneasiness.

"Sir," he hollered. "It's me, Chap. Where are you?"

There was silence.

"Answer me. Where are you?"

Chap called again and again, listening for an answer each time.

"Can I help?"

Chap jumped and whirled around. Erica was standing beside her bicycle. He hadn't heard her ride up.

"I'm sorry. I didn't mean to startle you," she said.

"I didn't hear you—that's all."

Chap stood, uncertain about what to say next. Actually, he had no idea about what to do next either, and the silence got very long.

Finally, Erica started to turn her bike around.

"I didn't mean to bother you," she said with emphasis on *bother.* "I thought you might need help."

She was on her bike, moving away, before Chap yelled, "Wait!"

Stopping, she looked back over her shoulder, apparently waiting for more than one word.

"Don't go yet. I don't know what to do," Chap said in a rush, surprising himself.

Erica pedaled back slowly. She stopped and put down the kickstand. Then she looked at him. This time he forced himself not to avoid those eyes, staring intently from above the scar that cut across her smooth pale skin. After what seemed like minutes, she looked at the car.

"I wonder if it runs," she said, walking around it and checking the tires. "The key's in the ignition."

Before Chap could protest, she opened the driver-side door, slid in, started the engine, shifted into reverse, and backed away from the edge of the ditch. Then pulling forward, she positioned the car parallel with the highway, shut off the engine, and got out.

When she looked at Chap and giggled, he realized his mouth was open. Though he immediately snapped it closed, his face felt lots warmer and no doubt looked lots redder, but Erica didn't notice—or at least chose not to comment.

"I don't think there's anything wrong with the car," she said. "Why would your father leave it like this?"

Why is he doing any of what he's doing, Chap thought. He'd had no answers about his father for a long time.

"I don't know, and I don't know where he is either."

"Let's shout again," she said.

They yelled and listened, then yelled again. There was no answer.

"We could check on the other side of the ditch. He likes the woods," Chap said.

Erica nodded. Chap scrambled down the steep bank to the dry ditch bottom before realizing that maybe she couldn't get down so easily, but she reached the bottom shortly after he did. They climbed up the other side and walked into the woods, calling over and over again then standing still to listen. The silence mocked them, unbroken by bird chirps or the rustle of the remaining leaves. Fear was forming a knot in Chap's stomach again, and he was having difficulty keeping his voice steady.

Finally, Erica said, "He isn't here, Chap. We ought to search somewhere else."

They scrambled down the ditch bank again. About half way up the other side, Erica slipped. Without thinking, Chap grabbed her hand to help her climb up the rest of the bank. Then for some totally unknown reason, Chap held onto it as they stood looking up and down the highway. Her skin was soft and warm.

"Maybe your father walked home," Erica said, dropping his hand and moving towards the car. "Come on. I'll drive. You ride my bike."

Staring at her, Chap said nothing.

"You can ride a bike, can't you?" she said.

He continued to stare, and she stared back.

Finally, he swallowed and said, "I can ride a bike, but can you drive a car?"

"Of course."

Her eyes had never left his face. She seemed to enjoy the fact that his face looked like it was on fire. Then she smiled—a wide, friendly smile—and the fire spread all through him.

"Okay. I confess. I'm older. I should be a junior, but I missed so much school because of the accident that I dropped out—after I got my driver's license."

Chap was still staring at her. She giggled. The sound made him feel warm and safe like he felt when Lori laughed, and for a few moments, he forgot why they were standing along the highway beside an old empty car on a November afternoon.

"For heaven's sake," she said, grinning, "do you want to see my license?"

Suddenly, Chap relaxed and grinned back.

"Race you," he said, grabbing her bike and heading for First Woods Road.

He'd just turned onto the blacktop when the car slowly pulled around him. Erica waved one hand. Pedaling furiously, he struggled to keep up. When she stopped in front of the one-car garage, Chap dropped the bike and flopped down on the brownish grass.

"Feeling a bit winded?" she said playfully, leaning over him. "If the door's unlocked, I'll carry in the groceries while you recuperate."

Chap scrambled up.

"That's okay. I can handle things now. Thanks."

Suddenly, he didn't want Erica to go into the house—he wasn't quite sure why. Maybe he feared that the loneliness and silence in there might swallow up the warm feeling he had with her outside. Maybe he was afraid his father wasn't there. Or maybe he was afraid he was. Besides, Chap wasn't sure whether he'd won this particular game or passed the test.

Erica's face clouded.

"Thanks for the help. Really. My father's inside no doubt, probably in the den like always," Chap said with false cheerfulness.

Picking up the bike, he wheeled it to her and said, "I'll meet you in the morning at the corner."

"All right," she said, her eyes brightening. "I'll see you tomorrow."

Heart pounding, Chap watched until she disappeared onto First Woods Road. Then he picked up a bag of groceries and headed inside.

Chap was walking up the back porch steps with the last bag, dreading the moment when he'd know for sure whether or not his father was in the den, when he heard Erica's shout.

Putting the sack down quickly, he raced around the side of the house. He couldn't understand what she was saying until she skidded to a stop.

"There's a man," she said, stopping to get her breath. "He's beside the road."

"Come on," Chap said.

He ran down the lane and onto First Woods Road with Erica following on her bike. A man was standing just beyond the next curve. Even from a distance, Chap knew it was his father. Seeing him, as Erica must, in what had become his "uniform" made Chap realize how strange his father looked. He was wearing a dingy gray sweatshirt, frayed at the cuffs, underneath one of the short-sleeved khaki shirts left from his military days. The shirt was bunched up in the middle, misbuttoned again, and a black tie hung unknotted around his neck. His jeans at least looked clean. He wore no socks, which was no small wonder since he continued to stash them all over the kitchen, and his scuffed black shoes were untied.

Running up to him, Chap said, his breath coming in gasps, "Sir, are you all right?"

"Home," he answered without looking at either of them.

"I don't see a bump, but do you suppose he hit his head?" Erica asked.

Chap shrugged as he reached for his father's arm. "Come on," he said. "Let's go home."

Quickly, his father spun away and began walking down the road, going farther yet from the house.

"This way!" Chap yelled.

But his father feigned deafness and walked on even faster.

"Damn it!" Chap said, starting after him again. "Home is the other way."

Reaching out, Chap grabbed his arm. With lightning speed, his father whirled and slapped Chap hard across his left cheek. Chap stood, stunned, with his arms heavy at his sides. Without a word, his father turned and began to shuffle back south towards the house with his head down and arms dangling.

When he disappeared around the curve, the lump that had been in Chap's throat came back, then dissolved into tears that filled his eyes and slid down his cheeks.

Erica dropped her bike and walked to him. "I'm so sorry," she said softly, putting her arms around him.

Without hesitating, Chap wrapped his arms around her and, eyes shut tight, rested his forehead on hers. They stood there together until his cheeks were dry. Finally, she stepped back to look at him, holding his hand.

"Are you all right?" she asked.

"Yes," he said, looking away from her.

"Does he hit you often?"

Chap didn't answer for a moment. Then with his voice shaking, he said, "That's the strange part. I never got spanked, even when I was little."

"Not even a slap?"

Chap shook his head. "All my father ever did was raise his eyebrow, and he yelled—sometimes so loud I'd hide in the attic. But he never hit us."

"Oh," she said softly, "something is really wrong."

"I know. I need to go home now," Chap said, but he didn't drop her hand.

He needed to go home, but he didn't want to go home. As long as he stood beside the road with Erica, he didn't have to face what was wrong there.

Finally, Erica said, "Should I go with you?"

"No, I need to go alone."

Digging into her backpack, she tore off a slip of notebook paper and wrote down her phone number. "Call me if things aren't okay."

When she handed it to Chap, he held onto her hand. "See you in the morning," he said.

"At the corner," she said, mounting her bicycle.

Chap watched as she pedaled away. Then he turned and headed towards the silent house with the blank windows that reminded him of its emptiness.

Picking up the groceries on the step, he forced himself to walk inside. The other sacks were sitting on the table in the kitchen exactly as he'd left them. Chap walked through the living room and up to the closed door of the den. Wiping his sweaty palms on his jeans, he knocked lightly. When there was no answer, he turned the knob slowly and pushed the door open.

Looking up from the papers strewn about on his desk, his right eyebrow raised, his father took a pipe from his mouth. Chap swallowed. His left cheek still stung from the slap. He wondered if the handprint showed.

"I wanted to be sure you were home, sir."

His father stared.

"The car—"

The right eyebrow flew up higher as his father continued to stare.

"The car," Chap repeated, rubbing his hands on his jeans again, "is in the driveway."

"Of course," his father said.

Then putting the pipe back into his mouth, he picked up his pen and leaned over his desk.

Chap stood in the doorway, waiting for something—not knowing exactly what. But there was nothing, only silence and the light from the desk making a small circle of brightness in the dusty gloom of the den.

"Sir, about this game, why did you leave the car?"

His father's head snapped up, his right eyebrow high again, his mouth tight and forbidding. He glared, hard.

Dropping his eyes to the floor, Chap backed out, closed the door quietly, and returned to the kitchen. Standing there in the middle of the floor, he tried to figure out if he'd passed or failed the test. Yes, the car was safely back home, but Erica had driven it. Surely, his father hadn't expected him to drive since he hadn't had the behind-the-wheel part of driver's education class yet.

It felt like the fire all over again—a dangerous game with no rules and no way to know if there was a winner.

Feeling a sense of deadening exhaustion, Chap put away the groceries, one item at a time—lettuce in the crisper, tomato soup in the cupboard, bleach on the washer in the basement, milk in the refrigerator, another can in the cupboard. When he was done, he sat down at the table and laid his head on his arms.

* * *

Dusk had faded into pitch-black night by the time he awoke. His stomach was rumbling painfully. Jumping up to start supper, he grabbed a skillet with one hand and a loaf of bread with the other. In minutes the cheese sandwiches were browning, and some vegetable beef soup was bubbling in a saucepan. When the table was set, he walked to the den again, stomach churning from more than hunger, and knocked.

"Supper's ready," he said through the closed door.

After hearing the desk chair roll on the hardwood floor, he hurried back to the kitchen and poured the soup into bowls. When his father entered the kitchen, Chap nervously scanned his face. It was expressionless. His father didn't seem to care that supper was over two hours late.

Looking at the soup and sandwiches on the table, he said, "Good, Lori."

"I'm not—" Chap began, but he was stopped by the hint of a smile on his father's face as he lifted his spoon.

Chap closed his lips tight to stop the angry words from tumbling out. Soon the rumbling in his stomach made him reach for a spoon. Chap ate supper in silence, forcing each bite past the lump in his throat.

After the dishes were washed, he sat down and stared at Erica's phone number lying on the table. "Call me if things aren't okay," she'd said. Chap had no idea if what had just happened was "okay," whatever that meant in their household.

About ten o'clock he tucked the scrap of paper into his pocket, turned out the lights, and climbed the back stairs from the kitchen to his room.

Chapter 6

As the first rays of light streaked across the eastern sky, Chap awoke suddenly, breathing rapidly, fists and jaws clenched painfully. Mercifully, the nightmare faded before his conscious mind could retrieve it. As he lay in bed, the sky changed from gray to lavender to dusty rose. He wondered if Erica liked to watch sunrises. When his alarm clock blared, he jumped out of bed, grabbed his clothes, and headed for the shower.

Fifty-five minutes later, he quietly closed the back porch door. Even with the early morning sun shining brightly through the nearly naked trees, it was cold outside. Chap zipped up his coat and pulled on gloves before starting to jog down the lane.

As he rounded the corner onto First Woods Road, Erica called, "Hey, you," from behind him.

Chap spun around. "What are you doing here?" he asked as she rode up.

"I convinced my dad I should bike both ways now since the weather will be bad soon. I'm getting all the exercise I can."

"And he bought it?"

"He did," she said with a mischievous grin.

They walked along with the bicycle between them, the silence broken only by the thud of their shoes on the blacktop, the raucous cry of a blue jay that rested on a scrub cedar branch, and the tuneless twitter of sparrows.

When Chap glanced at Erica, she said, with a smile, "I remember. You don't talk much to anyone."

With the sun on his face and Erica so close, the tension that had been plaguing both his waking and sleeping hours began to drain away. He wanted First Woods Road to go on for miles.

When they got to the wooden bridge, Erica stopped to look over the side at the shallow water. The many shades of green that colored the river banks each spring and summer had changed to as many shades of tan and brown. The fuzzy tops of the tall cattails that had gone to seed were almost within reach.

"I guess he was home since you didn't call," she said.

"He was."

"What did he say about the car?"

"Nothing."

"Nothing?" she said, her eyes wide.

"He didn't say anything about anything," Chap said, fighting to make his voice sound matter-of-fact. "No apology, no explanation. He acted as if nothing was out of the ordinary."

"So you aren't in trouble because I drove the car?"

"No. It was probably one of his games, but he won't say."

"A game? You're going to have to explain that," she said.

"He sets up situations for me to solve. Then he critiques my reasoning skills, at least he used to."

"And this time he didn't?" Erica said, her eyebrows raised.

Chap shrugged.

As they started walking again, the quiet settled in, but it didn't feel as comfortable as before. It was like his father's shadow hung over them, changing the peaceful feeling of silence to a troubling one.

After Erica pushed her bicycle into the bushes, they stood beside the stop sign at the highway. She looked solemn with tiny frown wrinkles between her dark eyebrows.

"I don't understand this game thing. Can we talk more on the way home?"

"Sure."

"And your father really said nothing last night? I find that hard to believe."

"Well, not quite nothing. At supper he said, 'Good, Lori.'"

Erica's face relaxed into a teasing grin. "So that's your real name. I knew it wasn't Chap."

"You'll never know," he said, smiling, "but for the record, Lori is my sister."

Erica's smile faded. "So why did he call you Lori? Was he trying to be funny?"

Chap hesitated, planning what to say about his father. *Funny* was not a word that came to mind, maybe absent-minded but definitely not funny. Erica's beautiful, intense eyes searched his face as she waited for the answer he didn't have. He shrugged again. Suddenly, he wanted to touch her face, to trace the scar with his fingertips, to take away the pain she must have felt. He wanted to kiss her.

But that would have to wait since the bus was rounding the corner and beginning to slow.

"What are you thinking?" Erica said as he gazed at her.

The blood rushed to Chap's face.

"Oh, that kind of thoughts," she said playfully over her shoulder as she stepped onto the bus.

Without hesitating, Chap followed Erica to a center seat, ignoring the hoots from a couple of the guys in the back. When he curled his fingers around her hand, which lay on the seat between them, she leaned ever so slightly until their shoulders touched.

* * *

After they parted inside the building, Chap decided not to go to his locker. Tom would find out about Erica sooner or later, and he'd revel in the teasing and the arm punching. Chap wanted to delay that because he felt too good and because Tom could be a real pain in the butt sometimes.

Chap was at the door to homeroom before he remembered the pencils he'd need for an algebra quiz. Back at his locker, Chap found Tom already there, rummaging through the clutter inside his.

"How are you doing?" Tom yelled above the noise of many voices and slamming locker doors up and down the hallway.

"Okay."

"I thought you'd call last night. Don't you have an algebra quiz today?"

"Yes, but I'll go over it in homeroom. No sweat," Chap said, feigning confidence.

"I'll see you later then."

"Later," Chap said, feeling relieved.

* * *

The morning hours crept—geography, always boring; algebra, always frustrating; Spanish, always foreign. Then Chap raced to fourth hour English, again wanting to avoid Tom. Chap was seated in his usual spot by the back window when

Erica entered. She smiled at him, making his heart pound, before she sat down in the front row. Chap enjoyed the entire class without hearing a single word Mrs. Hunt said.

When the bell rang, Tom rushed into the hallway as usual. Quickly gathering his books, Chap walked up behind Erica.

"Want to eat together?"

"Sorry, Chap. Mitzi is expecting me to help her with a history assignment. I'll see you on the bus."

"Sure," he said, smiling to hide his disappointment.

When he joined Tom in the hallway, Chap said, "Let's skip going to our lockers. I'm starving. I can smell the pizza from here."

As they headed for the fast food line, Chap decided to take the optimistic point of view. Not sitting with Erica would likely put off, at least for awhile, the inevitable teasing from Tom.

Chap's reprieve, however, was very short-lived. As soon as they sat down with the guys who regularly shared their table and before Chap had taken even one bite, Jason Grubner said, "Hey, Chap, we hear you've got a girl."

Chap dropped his pizza slice.

"No big deal," he mumbled.

"Whoa," Tom said, thumping him on the back. "You've got a girl? Tell more."

"Nothing to tell."

"That's not what we heard," Jason said loudly enough for half the cafeteria to hear.

"Confess," Tom demanded. "Who is she?"

"I sat with Erica on the bus. No big deal."

"Erica! Bird girl Erica? I thought she hated you."

"I never said that."

"But Erica?" Tom said, frowning.

"Yes, Erica," Chap said, his voice rising.

"Aw, Chap, you can do better than her," Tom said, his freckled nose all wrinkled.

"Knock it off," Chap said through clenched teeth.

All the guys at the long table stopped eating to stare.

"And you like her?" Tom's sneer was unmistakable.

Chap said nothing. Blood was pounding in his ears. He stared at the pizza lying upside-down on the paper plate.

Suddenly, Tom elbowed him. "I get it. I'll bet she's showing you something else so you'll forget about her ugly face," he said, drawing his finger from his nose across his cheek to indicate her scar.

Laughter burst out all around.

Chap stood up slowly and turned to leave. He was two steps from the table when Tom said loudly, "Maybe her . . . ."

Chap whirled in time to see Tom's cupped fingers jiggling up and down at his own nonexistent breasts. Without a thought, Chap flung his books onto the tile floor and slugged Tom in the face, erasing the sneer with the blood that gushed from his nose. Then Chap gathered up his books and walked down the hall directly into the assistant principal's office.

"Mr. Mueller, I hit Tom Thompson. He's bleeding," he said all in a rush before the man even looked up from the papers on his massive desk. "He didn't hit me. This is my first time in trouble, so I'll stay home the next five days and—"

"Slow down, young man. Sit," Mr. Mueller said, pointing to the blue padded chair in front of his desk.

Chap closed his mouth, swallowed, then perched stiffly on the edge of the chair. Sweat gathered on his forehead as Mr. Mueller pulled a paper from the top right desk drawer. Chap read Disciplinary Report upside-down as Mr. Mueller hurriedly penned in the date and time.

"Smith, isn't it?"

"Yes, sir. Chap Smith."

"You hit who?"

"Tom Thompson?"

"Where?"

"In the nose."

Mr. Mueller looked over the top of his little round glasses. He smiled. "No, I mean where in the building."

"Oh," Chap said. "In the cafeteria."

"Witnesses?" Mr. Mueller said, filling in one blank after the other.

"The usual bunch at our table."

"More specific, please."

"There was Jason Grubner and Deon Romano, Jack Hillegard, Troy Wong—"

"That'll do. Now the cause of the fight."

Chap didn't answer.

"The cause of the fight," Mr. Mueller repeated.

Chap said nothing.

Mr. Mueller looked up from the paper and sighed. "Come on, Chap," he said with barely the hint of a smile. "Please don't let me think you guys have gone completely nuts. I'm used to crazy reasons for fights, but it would completely devastate my belief that you young people do operate with at least some semblance of logic if you have truly hit Tom in the nose for absolutely no reason at all."

Silence.

"Please, a reason," he said again in a tone of exaggerated begging. "The form demands a reason."

Looking at the round ruddy face topped with curly hair, more white than gray, Chap caught the twinkle in Mr. Mueller's blue-gray eyes. Picturing him dressed all in fur from his head to his foot, Chap relaxed a bit.

"Well, sir, I had a reason."

"And?" Mr. Mueller said, putting the pen tip on the blank.

"I won't say."

The twinkle left Mr. Mueller's eyes. There was nothing Santa-like about him at that point. With weariness born from too many excuses and too many forms for too many years, he said, "Stay put."

Then he left the office, closing the door loudly.

Chap sat. The noise of his pounding heart mixed with the ringing bells, the banging locker doors, and the babbling voices outside.

Minutes later Mr. Mueller re-entered the room with several papers in hand. "Now isn't that amazing," he said in a distinctly sarcastic tone as he stared down at Chap. "You're absolutely right. You bloodied Tom's nose for no reason. Tom could supply none. Neither could your witnesses. You just stood up and slugged him right between pizza bites."

Sitting down heavily, Mr. Mueller began to examine a copy of Chap's grade sheet. "It sure seems like an honor student," he said before pausing, "well, an almost honor student—not so good at math, huh? Anyway, seems that you should have more sense than this, but apparently you don't."

Picking up his pen, he scrawled "No reason given" in the last blank space on the Disciplinary Report.

"I'll let you explain that to your folks. Get a copy of this from the secretary, and then go to your afternoon classes," he said, his eyes steely and his tone all business.

Leaving the office, Chap walked towards his fifth hour driver's education class and then right past it to the exit at the far end of the corridor. Hurrying, he strode off the school grounds and headed for the downtown section of Riverwoods about six blocks away. There he sat on a bench in front of the Triple S Café, his empty stomach rumbling as the aroma of the café's famous homemade soups, salads, and sandwiches wafted through the air when diners came and went. It was twenty minutes before a bus heading west arrived. The trip across town took a long time with the bus lumbering to a stop every few blocks to let a few riders off and another few on.

Getting off at the farthest stop, Chap began what would be a very long hike or, if he was lucky, his first experience hitchhiking. As each vehicle approached, he turned to raise his thumb, and as each sped past, he checked his watch, wanting to make sure he'd be off the highway and in the woods before the school bus passed by—not wanting to see Erica, not wanting to think about what Tom had said, not wanting to have to explain what he'd done to anyone.

The elderly man who picked him up about a mile and a half from the city bus stop talked loudly over the noise of the old, used-to-be-green truck. As Chap sat silently, nodding at the appropriate times, the old guy covered the bad weather, the fall harvest, and his wife's latest illness. At First Woods Road, Chap jumped out of the truck with a quick thanks.

Chap broke into an easy jog right away, his feet hitting the surface in perfect rhythm. He breathed deeply and regularly. He wanted to feel like he used to feel—running each morning towards school and Tom and the guys they hung around with and returning each afternoon to the big white house and Lori and their quiet father. Life had been predictable then, maybe even dull—thud-thud, thud-thud, thud-thud—but he'd slept without bad dreams and his stomach had rarely hurt.

Now he was running from Tom and Erica and the whole big mess at school, and he wasn't running towards anything pleasant in that empty house.

When Chap reached home, he went directly upstairs, tossed his backpack onto the bed, and walked down the hall to the bedroom at the far end. Opening the door, he stepped into the room that had once been Marilee's. Years ago Lori had boxed up the clothes that hadn't fit into the overnight bag Marilee had taken with her when she fled. Old sheets, discolored with age and dust, were draped over a rocker in the corner, a single bed, and a dresser, which had little bulges on top showing the outlines of a heart-shaped jewelry box and some perfume bottles. The walls were covered with the pictures of movie stars Marilee had collected, all faded with the bottom corners curled and the silver thumbtacks rusty from the moisture that stayed in the unheated, closed room year after year.

Chap raised the front window a few inches to let in some fresh air before settling onto the floor to wait, his chin resting on his arms that were crossed on the sill.

The sun had dropped to the top of the tree line across First Woods Road when Erica rode into the lane. Chap couldn't see her face, but she was pedaling hard as she approached the house. When she got to the front steps, the porch roof directly below blocked his view, but he heard the footsteps and the light knock on the front door. It was dead quiet. When Erica left the porch, he caught a glimpse of her as she took the sidewalk around to the back door. Again, she knocked. Again, it was silent. Finally, she returned to her bicycle and left. When she stopped at the end of the lane and looked back at the house, Chap had to clamp his mouth tight to keep from yelling her name. Then she was gone.

Closing the window, Chap left Marilee's room to the movie stars and the spiders that lived there.

It was thirty minutes before the phone rang, ten rings the first time, fifteen more a bit later. Then the phone was silent. His father was silent at suppertime. And the dark windless night was silent as the pale moon slid in and out of the thin clouds.

Chapter 7

If Chap dreamed, he didn't remember. Though his sleep had been long and deep, he didn't feel rested. His knuckles were sore, and his legs felt heavy as he walked down the back stairway into the kitchen. His father had already been there. Chap brushed the scattered cracker crumbs into the wastebasket and carried the milk glass smeared with peanut butter to the sink, wrinkling his nose in disgust.

He was going to be home for a weekend, then five days, and another weekend—nine consecutive days to spend with no one except his father.

Chap hoped Lori would call. She often did on Sunday evenings, and they'd talk, slow and easy, about the branch office in Virginia and her tiny apartment and about how school was going for him.

She'd also ask, "How's Dad?" and Chap would answer that he was fine, the same as always. Chap had never told

Lori about the fire in September or his father's silence or the socks and the napkin pieces showing up in odd places. All those were just his father's games, ones Chap hadn't yet figured out how to solve. Chap would have to decide what to tell her about the past two days. Maybe his father would tell her about abandoning the car himself. Maybe he'd explain to her what he hadn't explained to Chap. Then again there was the possibility that his father wouldn't talk to Lori at all.

The first time that had happened was maybe a month earlier. Chap had called his father to the phone in the kitchen, and he hadn't come. Chap walked to the den to make sure he was there. He was sitting as usual behind the big desk, pen in hand.

"It's Lori," Chap said. "On the phone."

His father didn't looked up.

"The phone," Chap repeated. "Lori's on the phone."

His father sat like stone, so Chap returned to the kitchen.

"Lori, he's . . . he's involved."

"Involved?"

"With his writing."

"Oh," she said. "But he's okay?"

Chap paused, then said, "He's okay."

They'd talked awhile longer, but the cheerfulness had left her voice.

After their father had refused to go to the phone two more times, Lori got mad, really mad. "What the hell, Chap! He can't be that busy. Is he doing anything around there except working on that book?"

"Sometimes he gets groceries on Thursdays."

"That's a real contribution," she said, her voice filled with sarcasm.

Chap had never known Lori to be really angry with their father. She was the one who used to make him smile, even laugh out loud occasionally. Chap had no idea why his father was ignoring Lori. She deserved a lot more consideration because she'd basically taken care of them both since she was just a kid herself. Actually, Chap had found out only recently about another responsibility she had.

One night when they were talking on the phone, he said, "We're not getting any regular mail, just junk. No bills from the power or telephone companies or for the credit cards."

"I'm getting all the first class mail here," Lori said.

"Why?"

"Because I pay the bills," she said.

"You!"

She laughed. "Calm down, Little Brother. It's his money, but I write the checks."

"Since when?"

"I don't remember exactly. A few years back. He kept forgetting, and I'd have to nag him. When they turned off the power that time—remember?—that was the last straw, and I've been paying the bills ever since. He has cash and some credit cards. By the way, have you still got enough cash left?"

"Sure. I don't spend much, just school lunches."

"Get a girl, and that'll change," she said, laughing.

"No love life here," Chap replied before saying good-bye.

* * *

My pathetic love life, Chap thought as he carried the breakfast dishes to the sink. He counted the hours from Thursday's handholding along the highway to Friday's smile in English class. He'd had less than a twenty-four-hour romance.

Chap didn't want to think about Tom and all the laughing faces at the lunch table. Nor did he want to think about Erica because no matter what questions she asked first, she'd eventually get around to asking the one Chap didn't want to answer—the one about exactly what Tom had done to earn himself a punch in the nose.

Briskly, Chap washed the peanut butter smears off the table then slammed the cupboard doors and drawers harder than necessary as he put away the dry dishes from the drainer. When he opened the farthest door to the left, two pairs of socks dropped onto the counter.

"Damn!" he yelled, hurling the socks against the wall where they bounced off soundlessly and fell to the floor.

Then without thought or plan, Chap took out every dish and glass and plate, looking for more socks. Before putting everything back, he scrubbed that cupboard inside and wiped down the doors outside. Methodically, he moved to the next one and then the next, scrubbing, drying, and rearranging. He tossed three more pairs of black socks into the corner.

Hours later when all the cupboards, top and bottom, were orderly and clean inside and out, Chap dropped onto a padded kitchen chair and put his feet up on another one. The light from the recessed fixtures in the ceiling glowed on the golden oak doors.

Soon the insistent rumbling of his stomach signaled lunchtime. As he made himself a bologna and cheese sandwich, he considered making one for his father as well, but after glancing at the little pile of socks on the floor, he didn't.

Later that afternoon Chap took down the red and white checked kitchen curtains and stuck them into the washer, not because he was still angry but because he was used to finishing what he'd started. He also wiped down the rest of the walls, scrubbed the floor, and washed the kitchen windows. It was dark before he was done.

As he and his father ate tuna casserole that night, Chap said, "I cleaned the kitchen today."

His father didn't look up from his plate. He continued to shovel in the bites, grasping his spoon with his fist like a small child.

Chap glared at him, remembering how his father had enforced table manners, remembering the thumps to his head whenever he forgot. And there had been so much for a little kid to learn—please and thank you, elbows off the table, mouth closed, legs still, back straight, no slurping, and no reaching. When Chap was little, he'd tried hard to please his father, but there had been many of those lightning quick thumps.

Dressed in frayed, mussed clothes, that same man sat, eating noisily. Chap choked down the bites of casserole.

* * *

Sunday morning dragged. About eleven, Chap went outside. The sunshine was veiled behind piles of light-gray clouds. The wind was damp and biting, hinting of the snow it would bring. Zipping up his jacket, Chap began raking the remaining leaves from the side yard to the rows of chrysanthemums that his mother had planted the year before he was born. They lined the walk from the front porch to the back door—the shriveled brown tops giving no hint of the splendid gold blossoms, which had contrasted with the clumps of lavender, purple, and rust only a month before. Dropping to his knees, he packed the leaf mulch around the dried plants as he'd helped Lori do in years past. When finished, he stood up to inspect the job.

Wouldn't Tom love to see him cleaning a kitchen and taking care of flowers, especially since Tom believed writing was the only unmanly activity that Chap enjoyed. Then picturing Tom with a black eye—or two—Chap felt better.

As Chap headed up the back porch steps, he heard the phone ringing in the kitchen. He dashed to the back door but stopped cold before turning the knob. Through the door glass, he saw his father standing in the middle of the kitchen with a pair of socks in his hand, staring blankly at the cupboards and completely ignoring the phone. Before Chap could decide whether or not to answer it himself—Lori wouldn't be calling that early—the ringing stopped. His father slowly opened a cupboard door, removed the jar of peanut butter with one hand, laid the socks in its place with the other, and got the box of crackers. Then after opening other doors and several drawers as well as the refrigerator, he managed to get a spoon, a glass, and the milk. He crumbled crackers into the glass, put a glob of peanut butter inside the rim, and added milk.

Chap stood outside the door, watching his father slurp the mushy mess. Milk dribbled onto his khaki shirt, which was already food-spotted. Cracker crumbs clung to the beard stubble on his chin. He sat, slumped forward, intent only on the glass. If he saw Chap, he gave no notice. Staring at that unkempt man, Chap wondered where the straight-backed, neatly dressed, ex-military man, who was his father, had gone.

Please, Lori, Chap begged silently, come home soon.

After he finished eating, his father rose slowly from the chair and shuffled out of the kitchen, leaving the mess. The door to the den slammed closed.

* * *

By late afternoon, Chap had reached a decision. When Lori called that evening, he'd tell her about their father—the silence, the socks, the fire in the den, and the abandoned car. He'd tell her about all of it. He'd also admit to slugging Tom since she'd get the disciplinary report anyway—mailed first class, no doubt. Maybe he'd even tell her about Erica.

As the minute hand crept past seven thirty and inched towards eight, Chap wiped off the stove and counter tops while rehearsing what he'd say to Lori. Later he sat down and stared at the phone, then the clock, and then the phone. At nine he got up to get a glass of milk and some cookies, but he was sidetracked by some smelly, fuzzy, gray-green leftovers in two containers shoved behind the milk jug. By ten o'clock the inside of the refrigerator was sparkling clean. Finding nothing else to do, he climbed the stairs to his room.

The phone hadn't rung. Nor did it ring Monday or Tuesday.

* * *

By Wednesday morning Chap was ready to go out of his mind with boredom, and he had five more long days to go. He tried watching daytime television, but the program choices were truly pathetic. His father was no fan of the medium, so there was no cable or satellite dish at their house, only an old antenna on the roof. Chap had clicked through the only four channels they received several times, rejecting inane talk shows, silly game shows, melodramatic soaps, and the local news that was local only if he'd been in Indianapolis. To make matters worse, for the first time in his life, he couldn't find a book that could hold his attention. He was antsy; his mind wandered. Even as bored as he was, he was careful not to begin cleaning any more rooms since he wasn't feeling that desperate for something to do. His father hadn't yet asked why he was home, and it was easy enough for Chap to decide to say nothing.

The weather had turned even colder, only in the upper thirties, and the intermittent rain muted the landscape to dreary shades of gray. Chap went out anyway to jog but came home shortly. The cold had bitten through his winter coat, and the icy droplets made his cheeks numb. There was no pleasure outside.

To make lunch last as long as possible, he took tiny bites around the edges of the bologna sandwich, watching the scalloped-edged circle get smaller and smaller as he slowly chewed each bite ten times.

When Chap could find absolutely nothing to do downstairs, he went upstairs, but his sisters' empty bedrooms seemed to mock him. Finally, he walked to the door that led to the attic, hesitating before turning the knob. The dim light from above barely lit the steep, narrow staircase. Ascending it, he easily avoided the steps that squeaked loudly—the third, seventh, and ninth—while remembering past struggles to step over those loose boards when his legs were much shorter and his breath was coming in gasps.

Chap hadn't been in the attic for years. The gray light from outside faintly illuminated the dusty shapes stashed throughout the large open area. He stooped where the dark unfinished beams sloped to keep from bumping his head, something he hadn't needed to do the last time he was there. Breathing in the stale air, he moved to the middle of the attic where a string hung from a single bulb. Among the piles of boxes and pieces of discarded furniture, the light revealed bits and pieces of his past. The solid oak high chair with the faded decal of a yellow duck—he could barely remember sitting in it at the long oval table, surrounded by his four sisters. Several almost-new, long, narrow boxes full of baseball cards his father had thought might interest Chap but they hadn't. Brown Teddy, his constant companion for so long the dark plush was worn away on the back of his head and his rump. The electric train which had tooted while circling the table in the dining room for years until Chap reached junior high and Lori finally said, "Enough! I want a real dining room." Two badminton rackets with some broken strings. A croquet set with bent wickets and chipped colored wooden balls and matching colored mallets. A huge stack of jigsaw puzzles that had filled the lazy hours of many winter weekends while his father's favorite jazz music played on the stereo and they consumed bowls of popcorn and mugs of cocoa.

His father's guitar. Kneeling beside the case, Chap carefully brushed off the dust with his sleeve before unlatching it. Inside, the golden brown guitar shone, as beautiful as he remembered it, nestled in the deep blue plush. Chap gently caressed the smooth wood as the memories washed over him. The walk through the quiet dew-covered woods not yet alive with bird sounds. The glimpse of a doe with white-spotted twin fawns. The warmth of a sister's hand that held his. The high bluff above Wandering River where they'd sat on a long flat rock they called the Church Rock. The sky vibrant with early morning gold and rose. The white Bible. His father's long, narrow fingers coaxing beautiful music from the guitar. The hymns they'd sung, his sisters' voices blending with his father's tenor, beautiful even later when there were only three voices—his, Lori's, and their father's.

Slowly, Chap closed the case. Rising, he dried his damp cheeks with his shirt tail and approached the low hexagonal window that overlooked the front yard. He sat down on the rough floorboards, wiped away the cobwebs from the window, and gazed across the colorless front yard to First Woods Road. Sometimes he'd huddled there behind an old cedar chest, hiding from his father. Chap tried to remember why his father had been angry, but memory failed him.

It was Lori who'd sent Chap up there for the first time when he was not quite five. One afternoon his father had stood towering above him, his body rigid with anger, his right eyebrow raised, and his mouth tight with fury. Ducking his head down, Chap began to move backwards, one small step at a time. His father's yell, "Stop, you coward!" brought Lori running. She stepped between them, then ushered Chap up the front stairs as their father continued to yell from downstairs. When his father climbed several steps after them, Lori hastily pushed Chap up the attic staircase.

Chap never knew what Lori did to calm their father, but Chap had scrambled up the attic steps other times before their father began to mellow, which was the way Lori described the change in him. His angry outbursts had become farther and farther apart until the raised eyebrow, during the past few years, was often the only remaining sign of disapproval on his otherwise expressionless face.

Lifting the dust-covered top of the cedar chest, Chap carefully removed his mother's Christmas album as he'd done before. Laying it aside, he reached deeper into the chest as he'd not done before, lifting out various bundles of letters tied with colored ribbons and some small boxes. He opened some of them to find rolls of yellowed handmade lace, old buttons, a tarnished silver baby fork and spoon, a collection of military pins and ribbons, and a wide gold wedding band. The letters were sorted by years, it seemed, most of them from his maternal grandmother, who'd died when Lori was a baby. As Chap was putting the letters back into the chest, one bundle, tied with faded red velvet ribbon, caught his eye. Carefully, he untied the ribbon. The envelopes were addressed to Mary Jane White from C. H. Smith. Chap ran his fingers across his mother's maiden name. Then he slipped a thin sheet of paper from the envelope on top. In neat, bold script, his father had written,

My darling,

I lie awake, still marveling that you have said yes. I count the days until we wed. I can imagine no greater joy than seeing your beautiful face before I sleep and again when I awake. Your smile warms my heart, your voice my soul. Someday, we will make babies together

and fill our home with little voices, love, and laughter like I have never known. You have taught me to love, and I will love you all of our days.

Yours forever,

C.

Slowly, Chap refolded the letter and slid it back into the envelope. He would trespass into their privacy no more. He retied the velvet ribbon and gently laid the letters back where he'd found them.

Then he picked up the album, opening it as he'd done often in years past to stare at the faces of his family in the annual pictures. As they'd moved from military base to military base, the living rooms changed and the family grew, but the decorated trees stayed about the same.

On the first page of the album were two almost identical black and white pictures of Charles Henry and Mary Jane, standing side by side with shoulders barely touching and little fingers linked. In the third picture, a blanket-wrapped baby was in her mother's arms. In the fourth, tiny, chubby Catherine Adele was standing between her parents. In the fifth one, Mary Jane was again holding a baby girl, Julianna Marie. Then there were two little girls standing between their parents. And so the pictures continued, but in color, with Marilee Bethany next and Loretta Elizabeth two years later until in the tenth photo, all four little girls stood between their parents—dark-haired, dark-eyed copies of their mother. For six more years, the Christmas pictures remained the same with the girls in stair steps inching upwards a bit in each one. The next one showed his father and his sisters as before, but his mother was seated, her stomach huge. Chap would be born the following month.

There were only two more photos in the album. In the next to last one, Charles Henry stood at-attention straight, even though he was holding Chap, his only son, in the living room downstairs. In the last picture, Chap, who wasn't quite two years old, was standing at the end of the line beside his mother, who again was seated—her face thin and her beautiful eyes shadowed by the disease destroying her heart. In less than a year, she'd collapse on the back porch steps with the chrysanthemums she'd cut strewn about her.

Chap went back to the beginning of the album, peering closely at only his father in each photo, looking for signs of change in him but finding none. His uniform was immaculate, his posture straight, his hair military-style short, his eyes always directed at the camera. Chap's sisters grew. His mother became thinner with the circles darkening beneath her eyes, but his father didn't change. For the hundredth time since Lori had left, Chap wondered where the man in the pictures had gone.

* * *

When the phone rang before five o'clock that evening, Chap answered immediately, all prepared to refuse an offer for a new credit card or for replacement windows. He wasn't prepared to hear, "Hey, Little Brother, it's me."

"Hi," he said, trying quickly to remember the speech he'd rehearsed on Sunday.

But there would be no need for it.

"I have positively the most wonderful news! I didn't call until I was sure," she said in an excited rush. "I've been chosen for a group going to London with Mr. Burris. We're going to set up training for employees there. Oh, Chap, did you hear? I'm going to England."

"When?"

"Next week."

He didn't speak.

"Chap, are you okay? Aren't you excited?"

But she went on without waiting for an answer.

"I know I thought I'd be home by Thanksgiving or Christmas at the latest, but who could've guessed I'd be chosen for this?"

Suddenly, her tone became apologetic. "I feel bad, Chap, really I do, leaving you and Dad alone for the holidays. But you two can get along without me a bit longer. You're doing fine now." The excitement was coming back into her voice.

"We'll have a wonderful celebration when I get home with all the gifts I'll buy overseas for you and Dad."

"Sure," Chap said, afraid to trust his voice for more than a monosyllable.

"Dad's okay?"

"Sure," he repeated.

"I've got to go. We're on supper break. The entire staff is working over tonight. Chap, you tell Dad. Okay? I'll talk to you more this weekend. I just couldn't hold the news that long. Bye-bye."

And she was gone.

* * *

The night was long and miserable with ice particles hitting the windows after the wind shifted to the north and the temperature dropped. Chap stared into the darkness, his mind reeling with images of the fire and the abandoned car and the way his father had looked when he slapped Chap's face. He tossed and turned. He needed Lori here—to take over again. His stomach hurt.

When he closed his eyes tight, trying to force himself to sleep, his father's blank ashen face floated in the void. Anger crept in to surround it. Damn that man who let his daughter pay his bills, keep his house, and raise his son.

And that was true. Lori was the only parent Chap had had for what seemed like a long time. He and Lori had always been close. In the past she'd always known the minute she saw him if he was angry or upset or frustrated or lonely, and they'd talk until he felt better. Why hadn't Lori realized he needed her? They weren't doing fine.

Chap replayed the telephone conversation. He'd said exactly four words—*hi, when,* and *sure* two times. She really should've known that everything wasn't all right.

But then as the storm passed and the moonlight peeked through the remaining clouds to give shape to the walnut desk beneath the window and all the clutter on top of it, Chap heard Lori's excited voice and saw her small face framed with the dark curls like their mother's and her large brown eyes. She'd be playing with a pencil as she talked. She always did that, bouncing it on the eraser or making it teeter-totter between her fingers. Her cheeks would be rosy since she colored as easily as Chap did, and her smile would be radiant.

How could he blame her for not knowing what he'd purposely not told her? How often had Chap said that their father was fine and they were doing all right?

Chap watched the moon as it inched from behind a cloud.

He'd been good at playing his father's games before. He could be good at playing them again.

Suddenly, Chap knew there was no way he could wreck this opportunity for his sister. Lori would be going to London.

Chapter 8

Chap must've slept because when he opened his eyes, the sun was playing hide and seek around puffs of clouds. Bits of ice, acting like miniature prisms, flashed with rainbow colors on the tree branches and on every blade of grass below as the sunbeams appeared and reappeared. But Chap wasn't cheered.

He arose, retrieved his wrinkled jeans and faded, misshapen sweatshirt from the floor, and headed down the back stairs into the kitchen. Ignoring the cracker crumbs and milk droplets that littered the table top, he filled a bowl with corn flakes, tossed the empty box towards the wastebasket—missing it by a good foot—and opened the refrigerator to get the milk. While he was emptying the last of the gallon into his bowl, he caught a glimpse of a gray plaid coat as it passed by the kitchen window. Before he had a chance to duck out of sight, Erica was looking through the glass in the back door. Chap froze. She smiled and gave a tiny wave. Chap still didn't move, painfully aware of his rumpled clothing, bare feet, and uncombed hair.

"Can I come in?" she said loudly.

After she asked again even more loudly, the years of manners training made his feet come unglued. Moving woodenlike, he opened the door. Erica looked gorgeous, her eyes sparkling like sunlight dancing on ocean waves and her cheeks flushed from the cold.

"Hi," she said.

Chap stared.

"You okay?"

He stared.

She raised her eyebrows and peered at him. "Are you mute?"

He stared.

"Do you know sign language?"

He shook his head as his heart thudded.

"Well," she said, unbuttoning her coat and pulling off her bright red neck scarf, "this is going to be interesting."

She's staying, he thought, giving a quick glance at the clock.

She noticed. "Yes, the bus will be at the corner soon. No, I won't be there." She tossed her coat across the back of a chair, then shivered a bit. "Have you got any hot chocolate?"

Chap relaxed just a bit. Hot chocolate. He might be utterly confused about everything else going on, but he understood hot chocolate. Then he stopped. The last of the milk was in his bowl, turning the corn flakes into a soggy golden mess.

"No instant and no milk," he said.

"It talks. Good," she said. "Have you got any tea?"

"Apple cinnamon or plain?"

"Apple cinnamon is fine."

Chap opened each cupboard slowly, praying no socks would fall out. None did. He got two mugs, the tea bags, and a jar of honey. By the time the teakettle whistled, the table was cleared and the cereal box off the floor and in the trash.

Erica was watching. When he set the steaming mugs on the table, she said, "I'm impressed. I know girls who can't boil water."

"That's sexist," he shot back without thinking.

"Sexist but true," she said, wrinkling her nose playfully.

They drank the tea in silence. The sun, shining through the kitchen window, danced around the wallpaper, illuminating the leaves and tiny red flowers. Erica set down the mug she'd been holding with both hands.

"I found out yesterday why you're not in school this week," she said.

Chap hesitated before saying, "Fighting."

"Yes, and I know why you hit him."

"You do?" he said, suddenly feeling very warm.

"Yes, Tom told me."

Damn it, Tom, Chap thought.

As if she could read his mind, Erica said, "He didn't want to tell me. I insisted, and with his nose so sore, he decided not to refuse."

Picturing Erica with her fists doubled up, standing over Tom—she was taller than he was, too—Chap started to smile until he remembered exactly what Tom had done. With his face turning red, Chap grabbed the empty mugs and carried them to the sink.

"No one's ever fought for me before," she said quietly.

Chap washed the mugs a long time and wiped the counter even though it wasn't dirty. Then finding nothing else to do, he turned around.

"Are you cutting today?" he said.

"Yes, I called in sick after my folks left."

"Why?"

"Sometimes a girl has to take drastic action to see a guy."

Heart pounding, Chap turned away to hide his flaming face.

"Want some cookies?" he said

"Sure."

Very slowly, he got out a plate and the cookies. Stalling to let his heart slow down and his face cool, he arranged the cookies in precise concentric circles on the plate.

Erica chatted on. "Besides, I figured you were grounded for the rest of your life—I know I'd be! I've got your English assignments, and I can bring your other ones if—"

She quit talking. Chap looked over his shoulder to see Erica staring at his father, who'd moved very close to her. Leaning over only inches from her face, his father said, "Do I know you?" which was the longest sentence he'd spoken in weeks.

"No, uh, no, Mr. Smith, you don't," she said with a stammer. Rising, she thrust out her hand. "I'm Erica Anderson."

But he was already turning away from her and shuffling towards the cupboards. Erica dropped her hand and sank back down onto the chair. Silently, Chap and Erica watched his father open door after door and drawer after drawer until he had the crackers, the peanut butter, a glass, and a spoon.

When he moved towards the refrigerator, Chap said quickly, picking up a nearby pencil, "There's no milk. It's Thursday, shopping day. I'll add milk to the list."

His father stared at the list in Chap's outstretched hand before turning his back and heading for the doorway to the dining room.

"Mr. Smith," Erica said loudly, "Chap and I can do the shopping today."

Chap looked at her with raised eyebrows.

She continued, "If you'll give Chap some money, we'll go to the grocery store right away."

Without hesitating, his father stopped, reached into his pants pocket, and handed Erica a crumpled wad of bills. As he left the room, he whispered, "Lori."

Chap looked at Erica, who was staring at the money in her hand. Her face was as pale as his was red. She dropped the bills onto the table. Then picking them up one by one and smoothing them out, she counted aloud as Chap stood rooted to the floor.

"Two hundred thirty-two dollars!" she exclaimed. "Anyone for lobster and champagne?"

Then she looked at Chap. "I think you'll need some shoes," she said.

"Wait," he said. "Driving his car once without making him mad is one thing. But twice?"

"No problem. I've got Ole Blue."

Chap stared at her.

"Ole Blue," she repeated. "Dad's pick-up truck with about a million miles on the speedometer."

"Oh," Chap said.

"I've had the truck all week. They say it's too cold for me to bike even if I do need the exercise. So are you coming with me?" Then without waiting for his answer, she added with a grin, "Ole Blue isn't glamorous, but she runs."

Chap grinned back. "Oh, yes! I'm out of here just as soon as I get cleaned up."

Her smile fading, she glanced at the doorway and said, "May I come with you? I'll close my eyes while you dress."

Understanding her reluctance to face his father again, Chap grabbed her hand and pulled her to the stairway.

* * *

With hot water cascading over him, Chap kept blinking his eyes to be certain he was awake. Even after drying off and dressing, he was afraid to look into his room for fear she would've evaporated into a dream. But she was there, standing by the window that overlooked the trees in their side yard, the gently upward sloping grassy area and the woods beyond.

Mrs. Hunt frowned on trite, overworked expressions, but at that moment his heart skipped a beat—cliché or not. He stood in the doorway awhile, enjoying Erica's pleasure as she looked at the sparkling winter view from the window. When he walked up behind her, she took his hand, and they watched the splinters of rainbow jump from one bit of ice to another.

"This is going to be a good day," she said finally, and his heart lost more beats.

Downstairs they grabbed their coats and went outside. Guessing that Chap might be grounded, Erica had parked Ole Blue down by the mailbox so as not to announce her arrival. When they started down the lane, she took his arm for support, explaining that her leg had been aching during the past week. Chap was sorry her leg hurt, but he liked to feel her so close since he still couldn't believe she was there at all.

* * *

Erica drove to a strip mall near the Wandering River Community College campus, where they'd blend in more than anywhere else in Riverwoods. There was no use in Erica pushing her luck and getting caught ditching.

"I'll have to go back to school tomorrow," she said as they pushed the cart through the grocery store, "but I can come over Saturday and cook lunch."

"You bet," Chap said.

They selected chicken breasts, pasta, and mixed vegetables for Saturday's lunch as well as hamburger and all kinds of fresh veggies for the anything-you've-got-to-put-in-it goulash she was going to teach him to make. Shopping with his father—or even Lori—had never made him feel so good.

After loading the groceries, they walked around the campus awhile before going to a little deli, where they ordered Reuben sandwiches and bowls of homemade beef and noodle soup. With Erica across from him and with noisy college students and loud, cheerful music surrounding them, Chap relaxed. For once in his life, it was easy to talk to someone besides Lori.

Erica wanted to know more about the games his father played, so Chap told her about the first one he remembered. It was Easter the year he was in first grade. Just before dawn, his father had led Lori, Marilee—she was still home that spring—and him through the grassy clearing and into the woods where a faint path led upwards to the Church Rock overlooking Wandering River. Sitting close together, they held hands while the sun emerged from the horizon in a burst of color. Then his father read from a white Bible, and they sang hymns accompanied by his father playing the guitar. It was their special church, his father said, one truly made by God, one they visited anytime, not just on Sundays.

That Sunday Chap had been eager to get back to the house because he was certain the Easter bunny had come. But though he searched and searched for hidden treasures, he found nothing. When he was close to tears, his father said, "Well, what do you know about the Easter bunny?"

When Chap admitted he didn't know much at all, his father suggested that some research might help. Chap had heard his father say those words to his sisters many times, so he headed for the living room where all the reference books were kept. He found the *E* volume of *World Book* by himself, but since he was only beginning to read, Lori helped him find Easter.

Stuck between the pages was a note from the Easter bunny, addressed to Chap and printed so that he could figure out most of the words. The note was the first clue in a long series of numbered clues, each one leading him to the next one. Chap had to look where it could be very hot, which was the oven; where it might be wet, that turned out to be the bathtub; where it was green and purple, which was under a pot of violets on the sill of the bay window in the living room. The notes sent him from the basement to the attic for over an hour until he finally found his Easter basket, brimming with goodies, in the trunk of the car.

"I can remember my father looking so pleased with me," Chap said. "And I'd had such a good time I put all the notes back in order and repeated the search that afternoon."

"That kind of game sounds more like fun than anything else," Erica said.

"They were fun, and I was so naïve that it was several years before I realized that other fathers didn't play such games with their kids."

Laughing, they pulled on their coats and left the deli. As they walked to a little park that bordered the river, Chap told Erica about anagrams. Sometimes he'd find a group of letter tiles on the table when he got home from school. He'd have to figure out the message in order to get the treat the letters spelled—a piece of cake or a chocolate bar or a dollar or even a movie in Riverwoods.

Returning to the truck, Chap also told Erica about the games that were physical. He might have to figure out a way to move a large object or to find something his father had hidden. One of his favorites was identifying the sounds in the woods while he sat blindfolded beside his father. In those days, his father had talked a lot. He hadn't smiled much even then, but Chap had always known whether or not he'd succeeded in meeting his father's standards.

Telling Erica about the games reminded him of a part of his life which didn't seem to be related to the present. Chap didn't often think of his father as more than the silent man with the raised eyebrow who spent all of his time in the den, writing the book that seemed to have no end. As they drove away from Riverwoods, Chap snuggled back into the memories he'd shared with Erica.

* * *

Back at the house, Chap put away the groceries while Erica sat at the dining table, resting her leg on a pillow. Then he suggested they go up to his room since he didn't want a confrontation with his father to ruin a perfect day.

Erica sat on the bed, her back against the walnut headboard and her legs stretched out on an old colorful quilt made up of over six hundred little triangles. Chap sprawled across the foot.

"It's your turn to reminisce," he said. "There's got to be something unusual about your family, not that any family could be as weird as mine."

She laughed. "Well, we don't play your kind of games, just cutthroat Scrabble."

She was quiet awhile.

"I guess the way my parents got together is different."

"How's that?"

"They were next-door neighbors in Chicago until they finished high school."

"Childhood sweethearts," Chap said.

"No, that's what makes it different. My mom's three years younger. She played with my dad's sister, who was her age. Basically, my parents ignored each other—or argued when the girls did things like listening in on his phone calls on the upstairs extension or getting into his room when he wasn't home and drawing mustaches on his pinups. My dad can recite a whole list of the girls' sins that he frowns about and my mom and Aunt Janet laugh about.

"Then the spring of my dad's senior year, his girlfriend dumped him three days before the prom, and in desperation, he asked my mom to go." Erica giggled. "Every time he tells the story, my mom hits him when he says 'in desperation.' Anyway, she claims she got the last prom dress in the entire city—an ugly green thing with a lot of frills. But the evening couldn't have been too big a disaster because afterwards they dated until he left for the navy at the end of the summer. For awhile they wrote letters, but the time between letters got longer and longer until they quit writing all together about the time my mother graduated from high school.

"She went to college to become a nurse. He stayed in the navy and met a girl in San Diego. He doesn't talk much about her, but Mom calls her 'that party girl' since she always wanted to be doing something fun. Whenever he was in port, they skied in the mountains or hit the tourist attractions in Southern California or went to Las Vegas. I guess Dad loved that at first, but after they married, he wanted to settle down. She didn't. Three years later, they listed all their possessions on a big legal pad, split them up fairly, got a quickie divorce, and promised to write each other every Christmas—which they have done.

"My dad stayed in California until my grandpa got sick. Then he came back to Chicago, where he met my mom again. It was then she realized he was adamantly anti-smoking. He had remarked that he was glad she hadn't continued to smoke despite having sneaked cigarettes with Janet when they were kids."

"But she did smoke?" Chap said.

"Yes, she got hooked while under pressure in nursing school—no irony there—but she didn't tell him. Then after Grandpa got better, Dad returned to California, and the letter writing resumed. A month or so later, he flew back one weekend to surprise her. When he showed up at the hospital at the end of my mom's shift, he saw her in the parking lot with a cigarette in her hand. He was furious that she hadn't told him the truth. She was hurt that her smoking mattered more than she did. They fought. He took the next flight back to California."

"Obviously, that's not the end of the story," Chap said.

"They won't tell me the details, but there were lots more letters and phone calls."

"And your mom still smokes?"

"No, she smoked her last cigarette outside the church about five minutes before she walked inside to get married." Erica giggled. "When they tell the story, I always say to Mom, 'No pressure there.'"

As they sat awhile without talking, Chap wondered what it would've been like if his mother had lived. He tried so hard sometimes to find a memory of her tucked away in his brain, a memory separate from the pictures in the attic. But he found none.

Erica broke the silence. Pointing to "Loss," which was lying face up on the desk, she asked, "May I read the rest of your autobiography?"

Without answering, Chap handed it to her.

When she finished reading, she laid the paper down slowly.

"I've got to go home now to make it look like I've been in school," she said.

"You'll come after school tomorrow?"

She nodded.

Chap followed Erica down the stairs, knowing that in moments the door would close and gloom would settle over the house again.

After putting on her coat, Erica turned to him. "Don't be lonely," she whispered, leaning forward to kiss his cheek.

Then she was gone.

* * *

In bed that night, Chap replayed the day over and over, but each time the shopping, the walk, and the lunch got shorter as he rushed to remember the time in his room—the warmth of her so near—and the kiss.

When he finally slept, he dreamed of Erica.

* * *

Friday crawled even though Chap had quite a lot to do. First, he spent a couple of hours reading the English assignments Mrs. Hunt had sent. There was a note tucked inside the book.

Well, Chap, you picked a good week to be gone since I've given no tests or quizzes. Your average is not in jeopardy. Do read the assignments though. Mrs. H.

After lunch Chap made a list of things he needed to talk over with Lori. At the top was having enough cash for groceries. Chap had no idea if his father had more money than what he'd given them for the grocery shopping. That would last awhile longer but certainly not until Lori got home.

In addition, Chap decided to explain the suspension—exactly what Tom had said and done. But Chap decided against telling Lori about their father's behavior since his father would be all right as soon as she got home. Besides, no lasting harm had been done. The school thing was different because it would be on his record. Chap also decided to tell Lori about Erica. Lori would be glad he had a friend.

After making his bed military style the way his father had taught him and straightening his room, Chap paced around the kitchen. There was still over an hour until Erica would arrive. Cookies, he thought when his stomach rumbled, snickerdoodles. He'd helped Lori bake when he was little. How difficult could it be?

After considerable searching, Chap found his mother's recipe in an old flowered file box and the cream of tartar, cinnamon, and vanilla crammed into the back of a cupboard. Then he got out the other ingredients, measured everything carefully, and mixed. Finally, he rolled the dough into little balls, coated each with cinnamon and sugar, and lined them up on the cookie sheets.

He was checking the progress of the last tray in the oven when Erica knocked on the back door. Whirling around, he bumped the flour canister with his elbow, causing it to teeter on the edge of the counter. He dove for it but missed. It flipped over, dumping flour in a big dusty white cloud all over him and the floor. Erica shrieked with laughter.

Slowly, he brushed the flour off his shirt, succeeding only in raising a new white cloud. With a towel, he made a vain attempt to clean his face. Then leaving a trail of white sneaker prints, he opened the back door. Erica's mouth was pinched tight, but the corners were moving anyway. When she reached up to brush some flour off his cheek, she burst out laughing again.

The smell of burning cookies broke the hilarity. The last tray of cookies went into the garbage, but the others filled the kitchen with the glorious smell of cinnamon—once the smoke had been aired out.

While Chap showered, Erica vacuumed up the flour, cleared the table, and made tea. By the time he returned, she was sorting out his books on the table. Glancing up, she started to giggle again.

"I'm sorry," she said. "It probably wasn't so funny from your point of view. You had to see it to appreciate its comic value."

"Glad you enjoyed it. I practiced all day to get it perfect."

"It was perfect, and the cookies are great besides."

Chap grinned.

Erica looked at the clock. "I've got to get going," she said.

"But we haven't had time to talk yet."

"I know, but we're going to the college tonight to hear a visiting orchestra play Rachmaninoff."

Chap had the presence of mind not to say, "Who?" Instead, he said, "Poor you."

"Not really. I don't advertise it around school, but I like classical music. We listen to it all the time at home. My music is like your writing, something you'd just as soon no one else knows about."

"Are you still coming tomorrow for lunch?"

She nodded as she pulled on her coat.

Chap walked Erica out to the truck then watched as it bounced down the gravel lane and disappeared onto First Woods Road. Back in the kitchen, the cookies on the table didn't look as golden or smell as good as they had before.

Chap flopped down onto a kitchen chair, elbows on the table, chin resting on his hands. The stack of books and the assignments Erica had gotten with Mrs. Hunt's help was intimidating—Chapter 6 outline for biology, long vocabulary lists for Spanish, several maps for geography, and pages and pages of problems for the dreaded algebra.

Oh, hell, he thought, I might as well get started.

Pushing back the chair, he headed upstairs for pens, pencils, colored markers, and paper and then downstairs to the refrigerator for an apple and milk to go with the cookies. With everything spread out before him, Chap reached for the algebra book and flipped it open. Between pages 114 and 115 was a folded half sheet of paper with "Chap" on the outside in Tom's blocky handwriting.

Hey, Buddy, I'll make this quick. I can be a real jerk sometimes. I need to take lessons from you and open my mouth a whole lot less. Anyway, I've talked to Erica—she's got real class—and I think she's forgiven me. The question is, will you? I hope so. This place isn't the same without you.

Tom

P.S. I know I used the word "jerk," but I'm kinda hoping you won't.

Grinning broadly, Chap refolded the note. Then he picked up a pencil to copy the first problem.

Chapter 9

Early in the morning, there were often moments before Chap's eyes opened when his brain began to sort through the nighttime fog. Sometimes it asked questions, such as What day is it? or What is that smell? or Why does my foot hurt? Slowly, his mind would begin to answer. It would identify Tuesday or bacon Lori had fried or a crash under the basket during gym class.

The next Monday morning, there was only a split second between Chap's mind asking What day is it? and his eyes flying open. The answer caused his stomach to do a tremendous flip. Chap's nine days of exile were over.

Throwing back the covers, he jumped out of bed and headed for the shower. The prospect of returning to school to face Tom and the other guys caused a whole thesaurus of emotions—agitation, fear, apprehension, misgiving, trepidation, and nervousness—all of which made his stomach roll more. But when he thought about the weekend with Erica, the thesaurus flipped to a different page of brand new emotions that made his heart pound.

Saturday morning Chap and Erica had studied together before fixing a chicken and angel hair pasta dish that caused his father to smile. Even though his father didn't talk during lunch, he did nothing embarrassing, and he wore a clean shirt—no matter that it was over a dirty one that was visible beneath the open collar.

That afternoon Erica asked to see the Church Rock, so they hiked through the naked trees over ground striped with sunlight to the high ledge where they sat with their shoulders touching.

"It's lovely up here," Erica said, as they looked at Wandering River and the small meadow below. "The climb was worth it even if my leg's killing me."

"What exactly happened to your leg?" said Chap.

"Let's just say I won't be wearing shorts again soon."

"What do you mean?"

"You don't really want to know."

"Yes, I do."

Erica opened her mouth to reply then didn't. She turned her head away but not before Chap saw tears fill her eyes.

"Sorry about that," she said finally, brushing her cheeks with her fingertips. "It's all kind of fresh yet. Not just the accident but all the publicity and the legal stuff."

Chap took her hand as they sat quietly awhile.

"The break in my arm was clean—"

"Your arm?"

"Yeah, he got my arm too, but it healed fine," Erica said, extending her left arm and waving it all around, "but my leg had a compound fracture."

"I don't know what that means."

"Well, the bones broke into lots of pieces and the splintered ends protruded through the skin in some places."

Chap winced and shuddered. "Oh," he breathed.

"Sorry," she said, "but you asked."

"I know I did," Chap said. "Go on."

Erica took a deep breath before continuing. "The first surgery was to put all the bone pieces back together with metal plates and screws. Later I needed more surgery for the skin wounds. If you think my face is scarred, it's in great shape compared to my leg!"

Erica tried to smile, but her lips quivered. Chap held her hand tighter.

"Then there was the newspaper and TV coverage—lots of it since the man was a wealthy, well-known business man, family man, community leader—you name it. They kept running the picture of him playing golf with a local mayor and two state representatives. Then he did the very remorseful bit for the TV cameras with just enough tears to gain him sympathy but not enough for him to be considered a weakling. I swear I began to feel that everyone was blaming me for standing at a bus stop—like if I hadn't been there, he wouldn't be feeling so much pain!"

"You're kidding, I hope," Chap said.

"Yeah, mostly, but there were some really dark days. And the speculation about a trial was worse because he was such an upstanding citizen with a beautiful wife and beautiful young daughters and a beautiful home." She paused. "He ended up pleading guilty, so no trial, but we went to the sentencing because I had to tell about my injuries. When the judge sentenced him to three years in prison, his daughters sobbed. And if that wasn't bad enough, his wife looked at me and screamed, 'He's a good man. He didn't mean you any harm. It was an accident!'

"One reporter had a great time with that slant on the whole affair. He portrayed the man's family as victims in one story—the wife, a stay-at-home mom with no work history, might have to sell their home due to the loss of her husband's income. Like we were supposed to believe that such a successful businessman had no other assets except a quarter of a million dollar home in the suburbs. And his wife had no clue that he was a drunk with seven other DUI arrests on his record."

"Seven!" Chap said loudly.

"Yeah, at least seven. But the guy was good at escaping consequences. When the DA's office investigated, they found two when he was in college in Ohio and three more when he was in the army stationed in Georgia, or maybe it was North Carolina. Anyway, he managed to get his license in Illinois without his record following him. The first DUI in Chicago was reduced to reckless driving, and the second one caused his license to be suspended less than a year before he hit me."

"And he drove anyway," Chap said quietly.

"That he did. He had over two times the legal limit of alcohol in his blood at eleven o'clock on a Saturday morning. Isn't that pathetic? He was an accident just waiting to happen—and I just happened to be the one waiting on the corner for the bus."

Erica quit talking awhile. The sun was warm on their backs.

Suddenly, she smiled. "Who could've known that any good would come from all that?

"What good?" Chap said.

"We moved here, and I've met you," she said, her blue-green eyes all soft.

The lump in Chap's throat was huge.

* * *

Sunday afternoon, Lori had called. She'd written down everything she wanted to discuss before she left for England just as Chap had. They took turns going down their respective lists as Chap added more notes to the legal pad.

When he mentioned their father's odd dressing habits, she said with a laugh, "Oops, sorry. I forgot to tell you to lay out clean clothes and his razor for him. Otherwise, he gets so involved in his writing he forgets to change or even shave. Remind him to get a haircut, too."

As they talked, Chap realized once again how totally in charge Lori had been for years, but it was his turn to shoulder that responsibility, at least for awhile. By the time they said good-bye, Chap knew how to survive the next couple of months without Lori, especially with Erica so close.

* * *

Glancing at the kitchen clock, Chap jumped back into the reality of Monday morning. Grabbing his coat and backpack, he headed down the lane. As he stood by the mailbox, all the good feelings about Saturday faded and all the bad feelings about facing the guys at school resurfaced. By the time the truck stopped, he was a wreck, complete with sweaty palms. Erica's first words didn't help.

"We've got a problem," she said. "Three strikes and you're in."

"That's supposed to make sense?" he said glumly.

"Only if you're an Anderson," she said, laughing. "When I started kindergarten, my parents made it a policy to meet anyone I talked about at home at least three different times. It was their way of knowing about my friends—or enemies. And guess what?

"What?" Chap said with minimal enthusiasm.

"I've mentioned you more than three times—lots more."

Chap's enthusiasm picked up a bit.

"So how would you and your father like to come for Thanksgiving dinner week after next?"

"I'd like that," Chap said with lots of enthusiasm since he'd been dreading the holidays without Lori. The idea of having at least one day of vacation with Erica sounded wonderful—even if it did mean meeting her parents.

* * *

When they got to school, Erica took Chap's hand, sweaty as it was, and they headed towards his locker. Tom was crouched in front of his, searching through the rubble that was inches deep and getting deeper by the day. When he saw feet on either side of him, he stood up slowly and turned around, his eyes wide. Only a faint tinge of yellow green remained beneath one eye. Erica and Chap stared at him.

Suddenly, Tom grinned in his best Tom Sawyer fashion. "Good to see you," he said. He raised his fist to punch Chap as usual, but his arm stopped in mid-air. Instead, he turned to Erica and offered his hand. "You, too," he said, shaking hers.

"Glad to be back," Chap said, smiling weakly and wiping his palms on his jeans.

And that was all there was to fitting back in. The teachers didn't say anything about the five days of unexcused when they signed his absence slip. The guys at the lunch table were the same rowdy group as before, and Tom was his old self, minus the arm punches. By the time school was over for the day, Chap was both relaxed and relieved. Besides that, he was happy because he was riding home with his girl.

* * *

As if the pre-holiday season wasn't enough of a rush all by itself, there seemed to be a conspiracy at school to load the students up with extra work. Mrs. Hunt informed the class that she was going to give them a real Christmas vacation and ruin her own by making a source-based argument paper due before the holidays rather than after them. At the same time, Mr. Ashanta, the algebra teacher, decided his classes weren't far enough into the text and began to double up on the assignments. Since Chap had managed to raise his algebra grade to a solid B, he was working like mad to keep that average. To make matters worse, the track coach was pushing Chap to try out for the team in the spring, so Chap was using the weight room during some study halls.

Then Erica decided that Chap needed some special education. One afternoon she pulled onto the shoulder of First Woods Road, got out, walked around to passenger side, and told him to scoot over behind the wheel.

"No way," he said.

"No, go," she said with her infectious grin. "I told Dad you had your learner's permit, and he said I could let you have some driving practice since you won't get any with your father, it seems."

"The truth?"

"Yep, I'm officially your adult driver—just a smidgen under the required age, but I haven't seen a deputy on this road like forever. So go."

Since Chap had never driven anything bigger than a riding lawn mower, his heart was pounding furiously. Even so, he put the truck in gear, checked the mirrors, and drove a whole mile and a half on First Woods Road without crossing the centerline or hitting a tree.

When Lori called on Wednesday evening to wish them an early Happy Thanksgiving, Chap could honestly tell her that everything was going great.

* * *

An hour before they were to be at the Andersons' house for dinner, Chap knocked on the door to the den. When there was no answer, he entered.

"Sir, it's Thanksgiving. You need to get ready to go."

His father said nothing.

Chap stepped closer to his father's desk. "Remember? Erica asked us to have dinner at their house today."

His father remained seated.

"It's Thanksgiving," Chap repeated. "You need to get ready to go."

His father rose and stepped from behind the desk. But he moved no further.

"I've laid your clothes out on your bed," Chap said, reaching for his arm.

This time Chap saw the hand coming and jerked backwards—but not fast enough. Though his father's palm missed, his fingernails raked painfully across Chap's cheek. Instantly, Chap raised his clenched fists, but he didn't swing. He couldn't hit his father, who just stood there—his eyes unfocused and staring, his face pale and expressionless— as blood dribbled down Chap's cheek and splattered onto his white dress shirt.

"You son of a bitch," Chap said slowly, unclenching his hands. "Stay in here and starve."

Turning away, Chap calmly strode out of the den and up the stairs to the bathroom. The mirror reflected his face, unnaturally white with three parallel scratches across his left cheek, one still oozing blood. The other two were angry red welts. As he took off his shirt, all the calmness seeped away.

His heart thudded painfully. His breath came in painful gulps. With shaking hands, he rubbed at the stains under the icy running water. He kept glancing into the mirror, half expecting his father to appear in the doorway behind him—wondering if he'd be able to force his way out of the bathroom before his father hit him again.

But his father didn't come.

It was ten minutes before the deepest scratch stopped bleeding. Chap stared at the mirror again. Instead of arriving on time with his father and looking presentable in a white shirt and tie, he'd arrive late since he'd have to walk, and he'd be meeting Erica's parents with a marred face and dressed in a gray sweater with sleeves so short they left his wrists bare.

Chap considered calling the Andersons to tell them he and his father couldn't come, but for the life of him, he couldn't think of a truthful reason. Lying was hard, not because of any personal superiority or even because it'd earned him a mouth full of soap a couple of times when he was little but because lying took lots of words said aloud as the person being lied to asked questions and the liar had to add more words to make the increasingly complicated falsehood plausible.

Chap could imagine the lies he'd have to tell. He practiced some of them in front of the mirror, listening for sincerity in his voice. "We can't come because my father isn't feeling well." Then "He has the flu, I think" followed by "His temperature is about 103" and "No, I haven't called the doctor yet." Finally, he might have to reply, "No, I don't want you to bring us dinner."

That last lie would be almost impossible to tell since he wanted to see Erica. He wanted desperately to see her.

Chap stared at the angry red lines across his cheek. To go or not to go. To hide his face or not to hide his face.

What the hell, he thought, turning out the bathroom light. His reputation isn't my responsibility.

Minutes later, Chap slammed the back door hard enough for the glass rattle.

* * *

The Andersons' log cabin house was set among the trees a short distance off First Woods Road. Time and weather had darkened the logs to a soft brown that blended with the naked trees surrounding it. The faint smell of wood smoke drifted on the November breeze.

Chap stood along the road awhile, trying to decide what to say to Erica and her parents. Then, without a plan, he walked to the front door and knocked. Erica opened it.

Chap said, "Sorry I'm late," as she said, "I was wondering what had—" She stopped and stared. Reaching up to touch his cheek, she said softly, "He did it again."

Chap struggled with the lump in his throat before he said, "Maybe I should go home. I don't know what to tell your parents."

"The truth if they ask," she said, taking his hand. "I'll go get them."

Alone, Chap looked around the inside of the cabin. The split-log ceiling of the living room sloped up steeply to the roof peak. On the right side of the room, an open staircase led to a wide balcony, which ran the full width of the room. Two doors opened into what were upstairs bedrooms. Downstairs, a huge fireplace of gray river stones dominated the middle of the living room. Beyond that was a dining area with a low, log-beamed ceiling and a table covered with a white lace cloth and five place settings of gold-rimmed china, crystal goblets, and silverware that sparkled in the light.

Erica returned with two tall glasses. "Cranberry cocktail?" she said, offering Chap one. "Mom and Dad will be out as soon as they give the turkey a final baste."

When they sat down on the soft blue sofa in front of the fireplace, Chap saw that her eyes were swimming in tears.

"What happened?" she said, taking his hand.

Chap looked at the glowing logs and bits of multicolored flames that danced around them because it was going to be hard enough to tell her without seeing those beautiful eyes.

He'd just finished describing the ugly scene with his father when her parents walked into the living room. Chap arose hastily to shake Mr. Anderson's extended hand. Erica had gotten her height and her dark hair from him, but it was from her short, curly haired mother that she got her deep blue eyes.

After a bit of chitchat, Mrs. Anderson asked about his father.

"For some reason, totally unknown to me, he decided at the last minute not to come," Chap said. "I'm sorry you've already set a place for him."

"Oh, that's all right," Mr. Anderson said. Then with a slight frown, he added, "I don't suppose you got those scratches from walking into a tree."

"No, sir, I didn't, but I'm fine, thank you."

Chap was relieved when Mr. Anderson said no more, and they both left the room to put the finishing touches on the meal. Erica snuggled up close on the couch as they watched the fire, surrounded by soft music—Rachmaninoff, she said—and by the delectable aroma of a dinner which Chap wasn't cooking for a change. He tried not to think of his father eating peanut butter and crackers in the big, empty house down the road.

* * *

After a long, leisurely dinner, Erica and Chap put on matching aprons—her idea of a joke—and did the kitchen cleanup while her folks sat on the couch to watch the fire.

Then they all played Scrabble. Chap had never competed with people who managed to get words like *zesty, hawker,* and *quiver* on triple word squares and who knew to add *–ot* to *jab* for another big score. He lost both games big time, but he still had a wonderful time.

After eating turkey sandwiches and more pie about six, Chap and Erica got their coats. As they were leaving, Mr. Anderson said, "We know you've got some problems at home, Chap. You can call here any time."

When Chap tried to thank him, the words failed to come. Mr. Anderson nodded as if he understood.

* * *

The house was dark except for the dim light coming from the window in the den. After Erica and Chap cleared the usual cracker mess from the table, they warmed up the turkey and trimmings she'd insisted on bringing for his father. Then she had to go since she and her parents were leaving early the next morning to spend the rest of the weekend with her grandmother in Chicago.

When Chap walked her out to the truck, he took her in his arms. "I miss you already," he said before kissing her for the first time.

After opening the door to the truck, she turned back to him. Her eyes glistening, she touched her fingers to her lips and then to his.

After that, she was gone.

Back inside, Chap went to the den to tell his father that his dinner was ready. He wasn't there. It wasn't until Chap had checked his father's bedroom and discovered that the good clothes were gone that his stomach began to have that all-too-familiar ache. As he searched the other rooms downstairs, even the closets and his father's bathroom, he called out again and again, "Sir, I have Thanksgiving dinner for you."

When he was certain that his father wasn't anywhere on the first floor, Chap dashed out to the garage behind the house. The car was there. His father wasn't.

Running back inside, Chap took the front stairs two at a time. He began the search in Marilee's room at the end of the long hallway. Minutes later he found his father in Lori's dark room, sitting stiffly erect on the edge of her bed, his hands folded in his lap. He was cleanly shaved and dressed in everything Chap had laid out except the dark socks that Chap would find, no doubt, in a kitchen cupboard.

"I'm ready, Lori," he said.

As Chap stared at his father, illuminated by the pale hallway light which fell across the bed, his fear—and anger—suddenly drained away, leaving him too tired to protest.

"Your dinner's on the table," Chap replied.

Hell, he thought as he stared at his father, I promised Lori to take care of the meals and the laundry and all the other chores, but I didn't promise her to play your games. If you want to call me Lori, I may answer, or I may not. If you want to hide out in rooms all over the house, you can for all I care, but I don't have to play the seek part.

With that thought, Chap left Lori's room. But as he walked down the back stairs into the kitchen, with his father following like an obedient pup eager for his supper, a bit of doubt gnawed at Chap's resolve. He remembered Erica's words when his father had hit him the first time. "Something is really wrong," she'd said.

Chapter 10

Monday morning Chap hurried down the lane to First Woods Road, head down in the biting wind. Shaggy, dark clouds were piled up in the northwest. A heavy layer of hoarfrost clung to all surfaces, changing the gray-brown of trees, shrubs, and grass to a ghostly shimmering white in the pale light.

"How was the rest of your vacation?" Erica asked as he climbed into the truck. "Lonely," he said.

"That's good," she said with a grin. "At least you didn't go shopping for a new girl while I was gone."

"Not a chance," he replied.

On the way to school, they shared details in turn about his boring three days of doing housework, studying, and hiking in the woods and about her exciting days of Christmas shopping and visiting in Chicago.

When Erica stepped out of the truck in the school parking lot, a soft moan escaped her lips.

"What's wrong?" Chap asked.

"It's my leg. I never quite know when I'll have this shooting pain."

"Do your folks know?"

"Not yet. It'll be fine."

But Erica didn't look fine. Her face didn't light up when she smiled as it usually did. She slipped her arm around Chap's waist to lean on him as they walked towards the school building.

* * *

The snow started to fall early that afternoon, clumps so big Chap imagined hearing them plop outside the windows in last period study hall. The flakes stacked one on top of the other, creeping up the glass from the concrete ledge outside. The ball field beyond was veiled in gray, and the far woods disappeared behind the curtain of snow. When the final bell rang, Chap met Erica at her locker, eager to share the season's first snowfall with her.

Erica drove slowly, both hands on the wheel, a slight frown of concentration between her eyebrows, as the windshield wipers laboriously pushed the heavy, wet flakes from side to side, leaving clear arcs for only a moment. Wind gusts buffeted the truck. Visibility was poor. Erica tightened her grip on the steering wheel.

"One accident is more than enough to last me a lifetime," she said as if to apologize for the slow ride.

But Chap didn't mind. All time with Erica was good time—even a quiet ride on a cold winter afternoon with snow moving across the highway in sweeps and swirls.

When they got to the house, he asked, "Can you walk a ways? I'd like to show you something."

"I think so."

Arms linked, they headed for the woods. The tops of the leafless maple and hickory trees swayed in the wind. Just beyond the edge of the woods, Chap took Erica's hand to lead her into a small clearing surrounded by evergreens. Inside, away from the wind, they were suddenly wrapped in stillness and the beauty of deep green boughs iced in white.

"Oh, Chap, it's perfect," Erica whispered.

When Erica leaned back against him, he wrapped his arms around her. They stood together like that for awhile with the snow falling in silence around them. Chap would've stayed there forever except that Erica shivered.

"Come on," he said. "You need some hot tea."

Erica fell in behind him, following in his footsteps, as they headed for the house. When they reached the edge of the yard, she said, "You know, snow is more than just beautiful."

"How's that?" he said as he turned around—just in time to get a big glob of snow square in the face.

Before he had time to retaliate, two more handfuls hit him. And the war was on.

By the time they got to the back porch, they were snow covered with crystals clinging to their hair, eyebrows, and coats. Laughing, they took off their shoes and shook their coats before opening the back door. Erica stepped into the kitchen first.

"Oh, Chap," she said, looking down at her feet.

"What's the—?" he said as cold water soaked through his socks.

Water was pouring from the kitchen faucet and cascading to the floor from the overflowing sink. Chap dashed across the vinyl floor, making little splashes in the standing water, to turn off the tap.

"What in the hell is he trying to do to me?"

Erica didn't move. She was looking at him, her eyes sad and teary.

"This can't be a game anymore. He's doing dangerous, harmful things," Chap said, his voice harsh and loud. "I'm going to ask him."

"Oh, Chap, don't. Not now," she said, moving between him and the door into the dining room. "Let's just clean this up."

Chap stopped, then stood there, staring, trying to figure out how to clean up that much water.

Finally, he said, "Let's sweep the water to the basement stairs. There's a floor drain down there."

Using brooms, they began to slowly move the water across the floor to the basement doorway where it trickled down and dripped from the open-back stairs to the concrete floor below. Sweep after sweep, they pushed the water across the floor to the door, going back again and again for puddles which had escaped.

Later Chap went to the basement to sweep the water there to the drain while Erica used a sponge mop to get up the remaining moisture in the kitchen. Then Chap set two fans he'd retrieved from the hall closet on either end of the kitchen and turned them on high to blow air from side to side.

It was after five o'clock before they stripped off their wet socks to dry their icy cold feet. Then Chap headed upstairs to get clean footwear for both of them while Erica called home.

As Chap walked back into the kitchen, he overheard her say, "I haven't talked to him yet, but I will. I'll be home soon."

"You haven't talked to me about what?" he said.

"I'll make some tea," she said, her eyes down as she moved to the stove.

Chap watched her get the mugs, the tea bags, and the honey as the water in the teakettle began to hum. When she stopped moving, she stood with most of her weight on her good leg, her other heel raised slightly off the floor. Something wasn't right. She wasn't looking at him or talking. After setting the mugs on the table, she sat down, pulled up an extra chair to rest her leg, and looked at him, her eyes sad again.

"I don't know quite where to begin since anywhere I begin will likely upset you," she said softly.

She stopped to sip her tea. Chap didn't touch his, and he didn't say anything either.

"Do you know what Alzheimer's disease is?"

His eyes widened.

"I—actually, we—think your father's behavior may be explained by it."

"We? Your parents?"

Erica took another drink of tea before she began to explain. Her parents knew about the abandoned car and his father's anger that day and Chap's scratched face at Thanksgiving. They knew that his father had given Erica all his cash for grocery shopping. They knew about the socks and his odd choice of clothing.

"My mother was a geriatric nurse in Chicago for about ten years," Erica said. "She knows a lot about Alzheimer patients."

"That can't be," Chap said angrily. "He's barely sixty years old."

Erica reached for Chap's hand, but he drew it away.

"I know. You think of Alzheimer's as an old person's disease. But middle-aged people can suffer from it, too."

Chap said nothing. He couldn't even look at her eyes anymore.

Erica reached into her jeans pocket and pulled out a pamphlet. "Mom said you should read this," she said, holding it out. When he didn't reach for it, she laid it on the table. "It briefly identifies behavior that may indicate the disease. You know better than we do how your father has been acting the past few years."

Erica stood up to leave. Chap didn't stand up to follow her, nor did he look up when she said, as she stood in the doorway, "You know these aren't his games anymore, Chap." Then she added what she'd said before. "Something is really, really wrong."

After the door closed, Chap sat at the table, staring at the mug full of tea until it disappeared into the darkness.

* * *

Late that night Chap sat in his bed, his favorite fuzzy old brown blanket wrapped around his shoulders. Light from the bedside lamp shone on the shiny cover of the pamphlet.

They have it all wrong, he thought. My father's writing a book, for heaven's sake. He's an intelligent man—a self-educated, intelligent man.

Without touching the pamphlet, Chap turned out the light and snuggled down under the covers to sleep.

But sleep didn't come.

The snow ceased to fall, and the pale moon emerged from the clouds to turn the night into a pale version of day. The noises in the old house seemed louder than usual—a groan from the attic above, a creak from a bedroom down the hall.

It was after midnight when Chap reached for his bedside lamp. With the brown blanket around him again, he opened the pamphlet, subtitled "Ten Warning Signs You Should Know," and began to mentally catalog his father's behavior—matching it to the warning signs, recognizing most of them.

Disorientation to time and place—not knowing how to get back home, for instance. It didn't take much imagination to match that one to the abandoned car along the highway and his murmur of "home" when they'd found him walking away from the house on First Woods Road.

Misplacing things and putting things in unusual places. The socks that still fell out of kitchen cabinets or showed up inside pans. The stacks of little napkin squares that appeared all over the house.

Changes in mood or behavior, such as rapid mood swings from calm to anger for no apparent reason. He'd hit Chap twice without warning.

Changes in personality. Same thing. He'd hit Chap twice—but never before. He used to yell when he was angry—but not anymore.

Difficulty performing familiar tasks and *poor or decreased judgment.* Wearing clothing on top of clothing. Not turning off the kitchen faucet. Letting the fire burn in the wastebasket. Giving Erica all the money in his pocket to get groceries. Forgetting to pay the bills some years ago. Not always getting groceries on Thursday.

Problems with language. Chap could hardly remember the last time his father had really talked.

Loss of initiative. Except for writing, his father was doing nothing—actually he'd done nothing for years. It'd been a long time since he'd been involved with running the household as he once had with military type attention to detail—weekly room inspections, penciled in dates for regular haircuts and oil changes for the car, the weekly trips to Riverwoods for groceries, the evening meal recitations.

Chap laid the pamphlet on the night stand. He turned out the light, but he couldn't turn off his mind. Images of his father floated in and out. His father dressed in a clean shirt and a black tie, even when he was mowing the lawn. Taking Chap with him to get a hair cut to avoid looking like they needed hair cuts. Reading in the old stuffed chair in the living room. Balancing the checkbook at the oak table. Demanding answers from each of them at the supper table about "What did you learn today?" Pulling a surprise from a bag on Reward Day. Measuring an ironweed plant with his walking stick held on his head. Quizzing Chap about the fifty states when Chap was in fifth grade. Strumming the guitar on the Church Rock as the sun rose.

When had his father first forgotten to grocery shop, Chap wondered. When was the last time he'd read from the Bible at dawn? What day did he first wear the ratty old gray sweatshirt which he now wore every day? What was the topic of the last report that Chap had given at dinner time? When had his father quit speaking in complete sentences?

Chap curled up tight and pulled the brown blanket over him.

There was his father then, and here was his father now. And somewhere in between much of his father had disappeared so very, very gradually.

Chap wondered if Lori was as oblivious to the changes as he'd been. She seemed to blame everything on their father's concentration on his writing. Chap watched as the moon inched behind some clouds and nighttime darkness fell over the landscape outside the window. He stared into the blackness.

The book. His father's book.

* * *

The red numerals on his bedside clock read just after two when Chap reached for the lamp again. Rising, he found some sweats and a flashlight in his dresser. Then quietly, he opened the door to his room and tiptoed into the dark hallway, feeling his way along the wall to the front stairway. The old house was cold and silent as he crept down the steps and approached the door to his father's den. Slowly, he turned the knob and peeked in. It was dark.

Slipping inside, Chap closed the door behind him and turned on his flashlight. He was alone. Being careful not to bump into the stacks of books on chairs and on the floor, he moved to the huge desk. The beam from the flashlight revealed a jumble of materials—notepads, books, periodicals of all kinds, mail—both opened and unopened, receipts, dirty dishes, pens, paperclips, several pairs of scissors, and a huge assortment of newspaper clippings. Starting on the right hand side of the desk top, Chap methodically searched for the book—or any part of it, lifting stuff on top to look for papers beneath. There was no apparent order to what his father had been doing, and there was no manuscript that Chap could find—no stack of handwritten pages, no typed pages, not even blank paper in the dust-covered printer attached to the computer, which sat on a separate table.

Slowly, Chap pulled open the drawers of the desk, one after the other, finding in each a jumble of papers of all sizes and types. The papers on top in each drawer were mostly short notes written on scraps of paper in a large scrawl, barely recognizable as his father's handwriting. Chap pulled out a handful from the top left drawer and sank down onto the desk chair to look through them more carefully. On most were dates or names or battles or quotations. Then he found one that said, "Lori gone." Two others farther down in the same pile said, "Chap A paper" and "girl pretty eyes." Another was a crude map that showed the route from the house to Krogers in Riverwoods. Going back through the stack, Chap looked at the dates more closely, recognizing the date of his mother's death, Lori's birthday, and April 15th with the notation "tax due."

In another drawer, Chap found a daily log from three years ago which started with the words, "I need to remember everything." On the pages that followed, his father had written accounts of his daily activities—Chap's and Lori's, too. Gradually, the sentences got shorter until the last pages were filled with brief lists of people and places from his life, sometimes with question marks beside them. There were no more dates.

As Chap thumbed through the remaining blank pages, a small picture fell out—a picture of a smiling little girl with a curly dark ponytail tied in a red bow and two missing top front teeth. It was Catherine's daughter. On the back, his father had scrawled, *Who?* He didn't recognize his own granddaughter.

The lump that seemed to reside in Chap's throat on a permanent basis got bigger. Chap flicked on the flashlight and turned off the desk lamp. He swept the den with the flashlight, still looking for anything resembling the pages of a manuscript. He saw nothing. He rose and approached the file cabinet in the far corner of the den, noticing a putrid smell as he got closer. The top three drawers were crammed full of papers like the desk drawers were, but the bottom drawer held a collection of food in various stages of decay—a package of bologna that was slimy and green, several slices of moldy bread, two mushy brown apples, a banana that was black and oozing through the skin, a shrunken hard-boiled egg mottled with brown spots, and a glass of curdled milk.

Chap gagged.

Holding the flashlight with one hand, he grabbed a metal wastebasket and tossed everything inside, not caring about the noise of shattering glass. Then in his stocking feet, he fled from the house and dashed through the snow to the trash barrel beside the garage.

Back inside, he scrubbed the drawer and the wastebasket with disinfectant he'd found under the kitchen sink. As he turned away from the file cabinet, the beam from his flashlight illuminated his father, who was standing in the doorway—his face ghostly pale in the circle of light, his right eyebrow raised.

"Why?" his father said.

Not answering, Chap pushed past him, his wet socks leaving a trail of footprints as he raced up the staircase.

Back in his room, Chap sat on the edge of his bed, his chest heaving when the tears came, slowly at first, then in a flood.

* * *

Wearing a pair of dark glasses, Chap waited for Erica down at the mail box the next day. The first thing he said as he climbed into the cab of the truck was "The snow creates quite a glare, doesn't it?" The second was "I read the pamphlet. Please thank your parents for their concern. I really appreciate it, but I can handle things until Lori comes back. We'll be fine."

And he said all that without saying Alzheimer's disease.

* * *

The next couple of weeks were some of the happiest Chap had ever experienced—except when the pain Erica tried to hide crept into her eyes and when images of his father and the book that didn't exist intruded into Chap's denial.

Chap and Erica were intensely busy with all the schoolwork the teachers were heaping on them and the shopping and the chores, but they were doing everything together, and that was all that mattered.

Erica decided Chap should decorate the house for Christmas even though he had nothing except glum thoughts about celebrating with only his father. She prodded and cajoled and teased, calling him Scrooge and the Grinch, until he went with her to buy some fake greenery and tiny white lights. They even got a short, fat tree that filled the living room with a woodsy smell. After they strung the garland around the doorways and added the lights, they decorated the tree with colored lights and the ornaments from his mother's boxes in the attic. Chap liked the effect with all the lights out except the Christmas ones, especially when Erica snuggled up close on the couch.

Lori recognized the change in Chap during one of her infrequent calls which had to span a whole ocean and a third of a continent.

"Is this love I'm hearing?" she said, teasing. "You've said 'Erica' twelve times in less than five minutes, and you've talked more than I have. That's got to be love."

Chap denied it, of course, but he liked the sound of *love* when Lori said it, and he liked the feeling even more.

But then he ruined everything.

Chapter 11

Chap and Erica had been studying in the living room for about an hour. Erica was stretched out on the couch with her leg propped up on a pillow, reading a chapter for history, and Chap was sprawled out on the floor, filling in blanks with Spanish verb forms. When Chap sat up to take a break, he leaned back against the couch to gaze at the colored Christmas tree lights which shone through the plastic icicles hanging on the tip ends of the tree boughs and reflected off the many ornaments. Soft carols sung by the Mormon Tabernacle choir added to the holiday atmosphere. He felt so at peace.

Chap turned to speak to Erica, but she was asleep. Quietly, he rose. Then he sat on the edge of the couch, being careful not to disturb her. He just wanted to look at her as she slept with the scarred side of her face turned away from him. The scar was so much a part of her that Chap had never thought about how she'd look without it. He gazed at her flawless, pale skin with a touch of rose on her cheekbone. Her dark thick braid lay against the blue sweater near the roundness of her breast. She was so beautiful.

"I love you," he whispered, leaning over to kiss her.

As his lips gently brushed hers, she stirred and put her arm around him. Then he kissed her in a way he hadn't kissed her before—a long deep kiss—and his hand, moving almost on its own, touched her breast, gently at first then more deliberately. He shifted so that much of his body was over hers. Pressing against her, he caressed her with a hunger which was new.

Suddenly, Erica was struggling beneath him. Forcing her mouth away from his, she yelled, "Stop it!"

Chap jerked to a sitting position, then hastily stood up. Erica's eyes were wide, her mouth tight, her breath coming in short gasps, her arms folded protectively across her chest. She stared. Rising, she snatched up her books, then backed towards the door, and fled from room—all without her eyes leaving him and all without a word.

He was still rooted to that spot beside the couch when the kitchen door slammed. If she'd shot him, he couldn't have hurt more.

* * *

That evening Chap stopped his work in the kitchen often to stare at the phone, trying to make it ring, hoping Erica would call to say she didn't hate him. But the phone didn't ring.

For hours that night, he peered into the blackness as the wind moved restlessly outside, trying to comprehend just what he'd done, fearing he'd made a mistake that couldn't be undone.

* * *

The next morning Chap began walking to the bus stop early. The landscape was ugly and gray, the air cold and damp, the wind raw. It would snow again soon. Chap began to jog. He'd need to flag down Tony, who no longer stopped at First Woods Road. As Chap ran, he listened for Ole Blue, not expecting to hear it come up behind him but hoping all the same. It was a hope in vain. Erica hadn't come down First Woods Road by the time the school bus rumbled to a stop.

"Riding the bus again, huh?" Tony said as Chap climbed aboard.

"Sure am," Chap said with the nonchalance he'd practiced while waiting by the stop sign.

Deliberately, he walked back to where he'd sat during the pre-Erica days. Ignoring the guys' quizzical looks, he launched into a tirade against English and algebra teachers. It didn't take long for them to take over the gripe session so that Chap didn't have to talk anymore.

By not going to his locker, Chap avoided Tom.

And he didn't see Erica until English class. As the bell was ringing, she entered, tall and graceful, even with her limp. When she sat down, without looking his way at all, her long braid swished then settled against her gold blouse.

It felt like hours before the dismissal bell rang.

Tom was waiting in the hallway after class as usual.

"I hear there's trouble in paradise," he said with a grin. "Confess. What happened? What did she do?"

It didn't take much of a shove to pin Tom against the wall. Standing toe to toe and looking down at him, Chap said, "My academic record really can't take five more days of unexcused, and your nose probably would prefer not to be bashed again, but if you can't keep your mouth off Erica, I'll be obliged to slug you again. You got it?"

That was probably the longest speech Chap had ever made, and Tom's reply was probably his shortest.

"Got it," he said, his freckles in dark contrast with his pale skin.

For effect, Chap stared down at Tom for another half a minute or so. When Chap stepped back, the small crowd of expectant onlookers that had formed a semicircle around them dispersed, likely disappointed in having witnessed a bloodless confrontation.

Chap headed towards their lockers, taking long strides so that Tom had to hustle to keep up.

* * *

The next day Erica didn't come to English class. Even though she hadn't looked at Chap the day before, knowing she wasn't there at all seemed even worse. Despite his determination to keep his eyes on Mrs. Hunt, they wandered often to Erica's vacant seat—its emptiness stabbing his heart.

* * *

After school, Chap walked down First Woods Road to her house as the sinking sun bounced rose and gold off the low clouds in the wintry sky. The warm living room lights inside glowed through the drawn curtains, and the smell of wood smoke outside was inviting. But Chap stood still just off the road until the evening light faded, not knowing if Erica was even there.

By the time he reached home, gloom had settled over the house—and not just because the sun had set.

* * *

When Erica was absent again the following day, Chap quietly asked Mrs. Hunt after class if she knew why Erica wasn't there.

"That might be confidential," Mrs. Hunt said, "but I'll see what I can find out."

When Chap passed her classroom that afternoon, Mrs. Hunt said only, "The call said medical reasons, Chap."

That evening, Chap started to dial Erica's number a dozen times, but he never finished all seven digits. He could think of nothing to say that would make her not hate him.

* * *

The last day before Christmas vacation, Erica entered class, wearing the blue sweater which made her beautiful eyes even bluer. Chap's heart did a tremendous flip—she was there, but she was on crutches. After handing a note to Mrs. Hunt, Erica moved with practiced skill to her seat. Chap silently begged her to look at him, but she sat down without a glance in his direction and propped the crutches up next to her. Chap stared down at an empty journal page all period. It hurt too much to look at the long dark braid lying against the blue sweater and to remember those eyes that had last looked at him in anger and that now wouldn't look at him at all.

When the dismissal bell rang, Erica didn't stand up. Instead, Mrs. Hunt took the seat beside her. Chap wanted to walk out close to Erica, but when they remained seated, he had no choice except to leave the room.

Tom gave Chap a questioning glance when Chap joined him in the hallway, but whatever that question was Tom chose not to verbalize it when he saw Chap's tight jaw and narrowed eyes.

In the cafeteria, the lunch table talk was mostly about everyone's plans for the two-week break. Since Chap seemed to be the only person who wasn't taking a trip during the holidays, he was tempted to make up an exotic destination, but then there was that problem with the lie getting bigger and bigger. It hardly seemed worth the trouble, so he sat in miserable silence with a false smile plastered on his face.

He didn't see Erica anywhere.

* * *

After the final bell rang that afternoon, there was even more pandemonium in the halls than usual. When Chap reached his locker, Tom slammed the door of his and walked across the hall.

"Hey, man," he said without his Tom Sawyer look, "don't get mad, but I want to say I'm real sorry to see Erica on crutches. I think she's a class act."

"I'll tell her—if she ever speaks to me again." Then realizing that he might've given Tom an opening to ask questions, Chap hastily added, "Don't ask."

Tom shrugged.

"Merry Christmas, Chap," he said without a punch on the arm—which was apparently a permanent plus to their friendship since Chap's return from the five-day suspension.

As kids poured out of the building, calling good-byes to each other, Chap walked slowly down the steps towards the bus. He was in no hurry to begin a long vacation with only his father.

"Chap?"

He whirled around. Erica was leaning against the building near the stairs, her face solemn and pale in sharp contrast with the jagged scar and red neck scarf.

"Can I take you home?" she said, her mouth tight.

Not trusting his voice, Chap nodded.

They walked far apart across the snowy parking lot to Ole Blue. Erica was quite expert with the crutches, maneuvering easily around the deeper piles of slush and across the ruts made by many cars. After climbing into the driver's side, she propped the crutches against the bench seat between them.

The silence was heavy as she drove through Riverwoods and onto the highway. Chap stared out the side window. The scenery was monochromatic, the grayness outside matching the gloom that settled between them in the truck. Chap was grateful for the noise from the old engine which drowned out the beating of his heart.

After turning onto First Woods Road and crossing the wooden bridge, Erica said, "Can we talk?"

Chap nodded again as his insides tightened.

Erica pulled into a narrow lane that led back to a summer cabin on Wandering River. Turning off the engine, she stared straight ahead, her profile stern and her hands still tightly clenching the steering wheel. Their breath made little frosty puffs in the cold as the minutes passed.

"I need to know if Tom was right," Erica said finally with strong emphasis on *Tom* and *right*.

Not knowing what she meant, Chap said nothing. The silence was long before she spoke again.

"I see myself in the mirror every day, and I know what I look like. Did you start spending time with me to get sex, figuring I'd be so glad anyone would pay attention to me that I'd be easy?" That last part tumbled out as her voice rose. She turned to stare at him, her eyes flashing angrily. "I have a right to know."

Chap could only shake his head as tears threatened to fill his eyes.

"You know," she said, "this isn't a really good time for you not to talk much."

"I love you," he said softly.

Her angry stare didn't change.

"But you didn't call," she said, emphasizing each word. "My guess is that since you didn't get what you wanted, you're done with me."

Working hard to speak, he said, "I didn't call because I didn't know what to say to make you not hate me."

Erica turned her face away, but he saw tears slide down her right cheek. He wanted to comfort her, but the distance between them was much more than part of a truck seat. Minutes passed.

"I've been in Chicago," she said at last, "seeing an orthopedic surgeon—seeing several surgeons actually. My leg hasn't healed right. That's why it hurts." Her voice choked. "I have to have surgery again soon."

Oh, God, he thought, I'm going to lose her.

When his eyes filled with tears again, he didn't try to hide them.

"My dad's staying here to keep his job in case we decide to come back when I can walk again. Mother's going to Chicago with me tomorrow."

She was crying openly by then, her shoulders shaking. After moving the crutches, Chap reached over and drew her into his arms.

"I'm so sorry," he said again and again as she buried her face against his shoulder and sobbed.

They clung to each other until the evening light was gone.

* * *

As the truck slowly rumbled up the lane, the headlights illuminated the front of the darkened house. A rectangle of pale light from the kitchen window fell across the side drive—with the shadow of his father's silhouetted figure in the middle. Chap turned away from the house to face Erica, who'd stopped the truck but left it running.

"It's not fair," Chap said. "You've already suffered so much."

"I know. I've been plenty angry these past few days."

"I'd do this for you if I could."

"I know."

Chap reached over to caress the back of her hand which was lying on the seat between them.

"I won't say good-bye, Erica."

Smiling through glistening tears, she touched her fingers to her lips and then to his—as she'd done once before. Then she said, as she'd said once before, "Don't be lonely."

Chap opened the truck door, then stood on the sidewalk while Erica turned the truck around and headed down the lane. He waited until Ole Blue's tail lights disappeared and the engine sound faded into the cold stillness. Finally, he climbed the back porch steps with heavy feet and a heavy heart.

When he walked into the kitchen, his father moved away from the window to stare at the doorway. "Lori?" he said, with a frown on his face.

"Lori is not here," Chap said, emphasizing each word loudly. He walked up close to his father. "She *hasn't* been here for months. She *won't* be here for weeks yet, maybe months."

He was ready to add "What part of that don't you understand?" but he bit his tongue instead. This pale man standing before wasn't playing games. Chap had to remember that. His father wasn't playing games. He was ill.

Half expecting his father to take a swing in his direction, Chap tensed, but his father ignored him—and his disrespect.

Returning to the window, his father peered into the blackness. Then he turned and looked all around the kitchen. "Lori?" he said again as he walked out of the room.

In frustration, Chap hurled his backpack through the doorway. If his father noticed, he ignored that as well.

All evening his father wandered throughout the house, upstairs and down, calling for Lori, missing her—as Chap was missing Erica.

Chapter 12

And that was the beginning of Chap's vacation from hell. And to make matters worse, no one seemed willing to let him stay mute about it.

Lori called three times in ten days, apparently feeling guilty about being away. Even so, she was having the time of her life, despite her attempts to hide it. In order to keep her from asking too much about things at home, Chap feigned extreme interest in England by asking her all kinds of questions. Having read *All Creatures Great and Small* and all the other James Herriot books in eighth grade, he actually did listen to her details about her short "holiday" to Yorkshire—she was sounding British already.

Erica also called. She was trying so hard to be matter-of-fact about the surgery, but Chap could hear the worry in her voice. When she asked about his father, Chap said only, "He misses you."

Chap didn't tell Erica about his father's newest bizarre behavior of wandering throughout the house, day or night, calling for Lori—the wandering that had started the night Erica left. Somewhere in the entanglements in his father's brain, Erica and Lori had apparently become one.

Sometimes late at night when his father's call of "Lori? Lori?" awoke him, Chap wanted to yell, "Hey, I'm here—you know, the son who's been taking care of things around here for months."

But he didn't yell—he didn't because he realized that even though he'd been handling things for months, he hadn't been doing very well since his care was minus the patient, understanding part. Chap was working on the patient, understanding part.

Chap didn't tell Erica any of that. What he did tell her was that he missed her desperately—and he loved her.

It amazed him he could talk to her so easily. Less than four months had passed since that day on First Woods Road when he'd said, "I don't talk much to anyone," and she'd said, "That excuses rudeness perfectly."

What an idiot he'd been. That rejection of her friendship then had cost him two months of happiness. Chap would've given anything to have that lost time with her at that moment.

When Erica called on December 28, the day before she entered the hospital, Chap knew she was crying, but he couldn't think of anything to say to make her feel better. He ached inside.

Two days later Mr. Anderson called from Chicago to say that the surgery had gone well, but they wouldn't know for some time if the leg would heal correctly this time and if the pain would be gone.

"Erica won't be back for a long time, Chap," he said. There was a long pause before he added, "Maybe not at all."

He explained about all the therapy she'd need again, but Chap hardly listened since "Maybe not at all" was ringing in his ears.

Before hanging up, Mr. Anderson asked about his father. Chap again ducked the truth and said, "He's fine."

Tom even called once, but Chap didn't have to lie to him about his father since Tom never thought to ask—hardly Tom's fault, if Chap were being honest, since Chap had never told Tom about any of the problems at home. Instead, Tom launched into a tale about the New Year's party he'd gone to with Heather, who'd finally noticed him. It was apparent that Tom hadn't had the vacation from hell.

* * *

Finally, school started again. Chap was probably the only person in nine hundred students and teachers to be happy about that. He desperately needed more to fill his days. His life had returned to what it'd been before Erica—when he'd been kind of lonely, yes, but miserable, no. But with Erica gone, what he used to enjoy he couldn't seem to enjoy again. The woods were too quiet, and his feet hitting the road when he jogged were too loud. When he tried to read, his mind wandered. When he wrote letters to Lori and Erica, his sadness was overwhelming. Thus school, even without Erica, would be better than being at home alone with his father.

When Mrs. Hunt asked the class to write about the holidays in their journals, Chap decided to tell her all about his father—all that he hadn't told Lori or Erica or Mr. Anderson or Tom.

That night he wrote for way over an hour, filling page after page with vivid description. Chap included that his father had been putting the clean clothes laid out for him on top of the dirty ones. At Christmas dinner, he'd looked fat and lumpy because he was wearing four shirts.

Chap explained that his father no longer spent all his time in the den working on his book—Chap didn't add that it was a phantom book which apparently had never existed. Instead of writing, his father was wandering all over the house. Chap never knew when he'd find his father standing in the basement by the washer or sitting on the front stairs or pacing the upstairs hallway.

Finally, Chap confessed to Mrs. Hunt that his father had even forced him to break the law—a dramatic way to start the last part of his journal entry, he thought.

Even though Chap hadn't planned on cooking a huge Christmas dinner, he wanted to fix something more special than tuna casserole, which had become a staple. Chap needed groceries, but when he handed his father the list several days before Christmas, his father had refused to touch it. Instead, he said, "Lori?" again and again as he looked all around the kitchen.

Chap tried two more times to get his father to drive to the store. He even said, "I'll do the shopping. All you have to do is drive to Riverwoods."

But his father wouldn't go.

The day before Christmas, Chap lost his temper. "Damn it, we're out of food," he yelled, yanking the list from the refrigerator door and waving it in front of his father's face.

Calmly, his father reached into his pocket. Then he hurled a wad of keys at Chap, who ducked right before a glass on the counter shattered.

Chap stood there a bit, thinking that his father couldn't really have done that. But he had. The list was lying on the floor, and the car keys were sticking out a bit from behind the dish drainer amid the glass fragments glittering in the sunlight.

His father, however, wasn't there. The door to the den slammed shut.

Chap grabbed the keys, his coat, and his billfold—which contained thirty-five dollars but was conspicuously minus a driver's license—and walked out the back door. With his heart thudding in his chest, he drove to Riverwoods, going not too fast or not too slowly in order to avoid attracting attention. Carefully, he pulled into a parking space away from other cars on the far side of the lot.

When he got back home, he carried in the few groceries that his thirty-five dollars had bought.

His father didn't ask for his keys.

* * *

Chap didn't include everything in the journal. He didn't tell Mrs. Hunt that when he baked a chicken for Christmas dinner and attempted gravy for the mashed potatoes, his father didn't acknowledge the effort with even "Good, Lori."

Chap also kept to himself that he'd driven into Riverwoods two more times. Frankly, neither movie was worth the fear he'd had of getting arrested for not having a valid driver's license, but he wasn't going to admit that to anyone either.

Even worse, he was now forging his father's name on the credit card receipts since he'd used the last of his cash for the Christmas dinner. No one questioned Chap at the grocery store when he used the credit card—maybe because he carefully avoided the lines with older check-out ladies who might recognize him from his trips there with his father. The card also worked when he needed to gas up the car.

But the card wouldn't work at the barber shop or the theater or the school when he needed to buy lunches. Chap needed cash.

It was easy enough for Chap to find the ATM card in his father's billfold "hidden" under his pillow—Chap, the laundry person, had seen it there often enough. He'd watched his father use the ATM many times. He even remembered the 8-8 that began the PIN—his father's birthday, August 8—but regretfully, he hadn't paid attention to the rest. When Chap tried using the 8-8 plus his father's birth year, the message was unmistakable, and he got no cash.

That led to another late night search of the den and the unlikely chance of finding a number beginning with 8-8. As Chap sifted through the jumble of paper scraps, Mrs. Hunt's words echoed in his mind. "It is correct to say that you have a PIN—not a PIN *number*, which is a redundant expression since that would be saying personal identification number *number*, and saying ATM machine is also redundant since that means an automatic teller machine *machine*."

With a faint smile, Chap continued the search, figuring he should get an A in English just for remembering that bit of information.

An hour later, he found the number written on the bottom of the map to Krogers.

* * *

Chap also didn't mention in his journal that his father had hit him again, hard enough to leave a bruise—not because Chap yelled at him, not because he drove the car without permission, but because Chap tried to convince him to take off his dirty shirts. Chap knew teachers had to report suspected abuse, and he didn't want to open that can of worms.

Only Tom had noticed the bruise when school resumed.

"Hey, what happened to you?" he said, reaching towards the dark spot on Chap's lower left jaw.

Instinctively, Chap jerked away.

"Sorry. I'm not going to touch you. What happened?"

Chap didn't answer.

"Come on, man. What happened? And don't give me that ran-into-a-door bit. You can't bruise your jaw there by running into a door," he said, pointing at Chap's jaw and grinning.

But the grin faded when Chap turned away to hide the dark side of his face.

Stepping closer, Tom said in a low voice barely audible above the din in the hallway, "Did your old man hit you?"

Chap hesitated while Tom waited with uncharacteristic patience.

"Yeah, he did, but it's okay. I can handle things."

Tom thought a bit before saying brightly, "I've got an idea. Why don't you come stay with me for a few days? You haven't been over since summer—and my dad likes you. He thinks I should follow your example. You know—study more, talk less."

Chap started to shake his head, but Tom interrupted. "Let's go," he said, "or we'll be late for homeroom. We'll talk at lunch."

* * *

By then, Chap knew what he was going to say. He'd had time to think and plan during a film in geography.

At the lunch table, Tom took a seat at the end of the long table away from the middle section where they usually sat, gesturing for Chap to sit in a different spot as well, one that kept the rest of the guys from seeing the left side of his face.

Shortly after they started to talk, Jack Hillegard yelled down from the other end of the table, "Hey, what are you guys talking so serious about?"

"Nothing important," Tom replied.

"Come on," Jack said. "Tell."

"Oh, I'm sure you'd be real interested in the project we're planning for old Mrs. Hunt."

Jack turned back to his lunch—definitely not interested in an English project for Mrs. Hunt or anyone else.

Chap decided that Tom, who could be so clueless so often, could be really smart sometimes—and a good friend who knew algebra and how to keep secrets besides.

After thanking Tom for the invitation, Chap explained that his father had hit him because he hadn't been feeling well—one of those half truths Chap seemed to be telling a lot.

"I really need to be there with him," Chap added, "until Lori gets back. I'm fine, really I am."

"You're sure?"

"I'm sure."

Picking up his hamburger, Tom dropped the topic for the time being, but he continued to extend the invitation until the bruise faded.

* * *

After Chap finished the journal entry the night before it was due, he reread the pages several times, relieved to have shared even some of the details with someone else. He slept soundly that night for the first time in weeks.

But the next morning as Chap reread what he'd written while he ate his usual raisin toast and banana for breakfast, he began to feel uneasy. What had seemed to be a good idea the night before seemed to be more a betrayal of his father than a description of the holidays. With growing uncertainty, Chap questioned the advisability of telling Mrs. Hunt so much. He'd always felt she was a trustworthy person, but did he know her well enough to be absolutely sure? Would his father become lunchroom talk in the teachers' lounge? Would he?

Hastily, Chap ripped the pages out of his journal, but before he dropped them into the wastebasket, he decided not to leave them at home—even in the trash. Grabbing his coat off the hook by the back door, he shoved the folded pages into an inside pocket.

As he jogged to the bus stop, he planned a new journal entry. Just before the bell rang to end homeroom, he finished a description of the little tree he and Erica had decorated with the ornaments from the attic.

* **

Chap's desire to have his time filled up turned out not to be as much of a blessing as he'd hoped. With semester exams looming in just a week and a half, the teachers continued their pre-holiday cramming. Every evening he had hours of homework as well as the housecleaning-cooking-laundry chores. In brief, he was swamped.

Erica was never far from his thoughts. He talked to her when he fixed supper, pictured her on the couch when he studied, held her in his arms as he fell asleep.

Outside the earlier snows melted, leaving behind only ragged-looking tan grass, shriveled brown leaves on tall stalks where wildflowers had once bloomed, and dark naked trees. The evergreens which dotted the woods seemed more gray than green, and even the bright red flash of a cardinal did little to brighten the bleakness.

And so the cold days of early January passed.

Chapter 13

January 19th dawned without any winter splendor or even a hint of sunshine for Chap's sixteenth birthday. As usual, his father was nowhere to be seen when Chap came down for breakfast.

Their relationship—if living apart under the same roof even qualified as a relationship—had deteriorated. Even though Chap continued to take care of his father, patiently most of the time, he came and went as he pleased. The first couple of times Chap had needed to use the car, he'd asked his father for permission, carefully standing more than an arm's length away. When his father had only stared, Chap decided he had permission, so now the car keys were in his pocket all the time—his father's credit and ATM cards, too.

For days Chap had reminded himself not to expect anything special for his birthday, but his heart apparently hadn't listened because he felt a distinct pang of disappointment as he stared at the empty tabletop. Surely, his father would remember his only son's birthday. But Chap was wrong.

After eating a birthday breakfast alone, Chap was greeted outside by a dreary, damp, bone-chilling day. The dark clouds hung low, pushed by the wind that made the cold bite through his coat. He was miserable by the time the bus rattled to a stop at the end of First Woods Road. The first wet snowflakes beginning to fall made snaky, watery trails through the dirt on the bus windows.

At school Tom was his usual self, rattling on and on about Heather. In years past, he'd been invited to Chap's birthday supper or to a movie, but without an invitational prompt, Tom had apparently forgotten also.

Later that morning, the wind lay and the gray clouds opened up, allowing large flakes to tumble out and cover the ledge beneath the windows outside Mrs. Hunt's room. When the bell rang forty-eight minutes later, there were a couple of inches of fluff nestled against the glass panes with the storm clouds promising more to come.

By the time the school day ended, Tony had to drive the bus slowly as it plowed though six inches on the ground and through drifts even deeper.

Nearing First Woods Road, he yelled, "Hey, Chap, it's terrible out there. Do you want to ride the bus home the long way around?"

"No, thanks, I'll walk," Chap said.

After the rumble of the bus faded, Chap stood in the middle of the road and pulled up his hood. He was surrounded by absolute silence as the falling snow muffled all the usual woodland sounds. There was no wind, and the snowflakes continued to float steadily downward. Chap began the trek home, trying to enjoy the peace of the woods but feeling isolated and lonely instead. His shoes made harsh, squeaking sounds in the stillness and left ugly indentations in the whiteness.

To cheer himself up, Chap tried to picture walking hand-in-hand with Erica, whose cheeks would be glowing from the cold. They'd marvel at how the snow iced each tree limb. They'd hurl loosely packed snowballs at each other. Then after making snow angels, he'd kiss her before they stood up.

Pausing to lean on the wooden bridge, Chap stared at the frozen river, the scene monochromatic with all the tans and browns covered in white. He missed not the heron but Erica—beautiful Erica who'd filled the empty places in his heart. Without her, the rest of the walk was long and cold with nothing to look forward to at the end except a dark, desolate house. Even the mailbox was empty.

Chap never bothered to yell "I'm home" anymore since no one ever answered. The kitchen table was still bare. After tossing his backpack onto it and hanging up his wet coat, he filled the teakettle and found a packet of instant cocoa. While the water heated, he sorted the homework into piles to assess the considerable damage it would do to his evening, not that he had anything more exciting awaiting him. Then with the cocoa steaming in a mug, he started working algebra problems.

Both times the phone rang, he answered quickly, hoping to hear a familiar voice on the other end, but the callers wanted only to sell replacement windows and tickets to a policemen's benefit.

Two hours later, as he fixed grilled cheese sandwiches and tomato soup for supper, he thought of Lori's sixteenth birthday when he was only eight. Their normally reclusive father had put on a suit and ventured all the way to Indianapolis for a day of shopping for Lori and an evening of fancy dining in a restaurant with a name long since forgotten. It didn't appear that Chap's "celebration" with his father was going to be comparable to that one. Chap shut the cupboard doors more loudly than usual as he set the table haphazardly. He was tempted to put a candle in the middle of his sandwich but decided against reminding his father. Let him feel guilty after Lori reminded him.

Chap went to the den to tell his father supper was on the table. When his father didn't respond to the knock on the door, Chap called, "Suppertime," loudly enough for him to hear wherever he happened to be wandering. Then Chap returned to the kitchen to eat without him as he'd done other times. Sooner or later, his father would appear.

After Chap finished, he cleared his dishes but left his father's soup and sandwich, both stone cold, at his place.

By the time the geography, Spanish, and English assignments were completed, Chap was feeling uneasy about his father's absence since he was usually hungry by late evening. Needing a break anyway, Chap headed for the den. When he didn't find his father there or in his bedroom, Chap's stomach began to knot. Turning on lights as he moved, he began a systematic search of every room on the first floor—checking inside closets and behind everything else. When he failed to find his father, he ran down to the basement. After failing again, he raced up two flights to check all his sisters' empty bedrooms, flicking on lights as he moved from room to room. He even climbed the squeaky stairs to the attic, breathing heavily more from fear than from exertion. His father was nowhere.

Heart pounding, Chap grabbed his coat and ran out the back door into air so frigid it made his lungs ache. Snow flakes were still tumbling down though they were smaller than before. The snow was mid-shin deep in most places—deeper yet where it had drifted.

The car had to be in the garage since the keys were in his pocket, but he looked inside anyway. Then he ran to the front of the house, his panic building as he called for his father.

In the dim light from inside the den, a single line of footprints was visible, leading away from the front of the house. Paralyzed with fear, Chap stared at the prints, which were already partially filled in with snow.

Finally, he shook off the mind-numbing paralysis. Racing back into the house, he headed for the basement to search for a big flashlight. Instead of a flashlight, he found his father's winter coat, lying on the floor between the washer and the dryer.

Oh, God, he thought, he's out there somewhere—and cold.

Quickly, Chap pulled his father's coat on over his own. Then, with increasing panic, he dashed back up to the kitchen where he eventually found a flashlight.

Outside, the footprints were fairly easy to see as they headed across the yard and into the grassy area on the edge of the tree line. Once inside the woods, however, the prints no longer went in a straight line. It appeared his father had circled around some, retracing his footsteps. The snow had filled the prints enough so that Chap couldn't always tell which way they pointed. Besides that, his own footprints were obliterating his father's.

Soon Chap was running in all directions around a group of trees, calling for his father, trying to see through the veil of flakes that chilled his face. Suddenly, he stumbled over a tree root and fell face first into the snow. Lying there with the cold creeping into his body, he fought for control, forcing himself to breathe in and out evenly. Slowly, he rolled over into a sitting position and developed a search plan.

After retrieving the flashlight, Chap walked straight from the center of the group of trees, where his father's footprints crossed and re-crossed, to the edge of the trampled area. Then he slowly swung the flashlight in a wide arc over the white, unmarred snow, looking for prints leading away from the area. When he found none, he returned to the center, walked straight out to the edge some feet away, and swept the outer area with light again. On the fourth try, Chap saw prints heading in the general direction of the bluffs. Bending over to see the prints clearly, Chap slowly proceeded upwards. Several more times the prints crossed and crisscrossed each other, but each time Chap painstakingly sorted out the direction.

As he climbed higher, his stomach began to ache. He tried not to picture what could've happened if his father had gotten to the bluffs and not stopped. Chap called again and again, but there was no sound, just whiteness and bitter cold.

Only a few yards from the Church Rock, the beam of the flashlight illuminated his father's body, curled up in a fetal position and dusted with snow. Chap rushed to him, calling, "Sir! Sir!" but his father lay still.

Quickly, Chap turned him over and shined the light on his face as white as death. Struggling to stay calm, Chap held the flashlight glass beneath his father's nose. When it fogged from his breath, Chap cried aloud, "You're alive."

But his body was very cold to the touch and completely unresponsive. Chap pulled off his father's coat which he'd put on over his own. Then struggling with his father's dead weight, he finally got the coat around him, zipping his arms inside without putting them into the sleeves. Squatting down, Chap hefted him into his arms, surprised that he could pick up his own father.

Then Chap started downhill towards the house, afraid to hurry since the deep snow made the trail slippery. Before long, his arm muscles began to ache from his father's weight, but he couldn't stop. Concentrating on each step forward—right, left, right, left—Chap prayed, "Please, God, don't let him die."

On and on he went, taking one arduous step after another—five minutes, ten, then twenty.

By the time Chap reached the garage, his arms were screaming from pain. Gently, he laid his father in the snow. It seemed to take forever for Chap's trembling right hand to retrieve the key from his pocket and put it into the ignition, but once he succeeded, the car started easily. After backing out of the narrow garage, he opened the rear door and propped up his father on the ground beside the seat. Then crawling across the back seat from the other side, Chap pulled and tugged until he got his father into the car. Finally, he dashed into the house. After pulling all the blankets off his father's bed, he ran back outside and wrapped them tightly around his silent, immobile father.

Jumping into the driver's seat, Chap carefully turned the car around and headed down the lane. First Woods Road was a solid stretch of unmarred white from the woods on one side to the woods on the other. Driving slowly, he watched the tree line on both sides in order to determine where the road might be. By the time he reached the stop sign, his hands were sweating. Jerking off his gloves, he slowly pulled onto the highway. Its condition was a little better since it'd been plowed earlier, but he crept along anyway, listening to the tires crunch through the crusty snow. His bare fingers ached as he clutched the steering wheel.

Chap stayed calm until the lights of the hospital appeared down the block. First his hands, then his arms, and finally his whole body began to shake. After reaching the emergency entrance, he leaned on the horn and prayed for help.

When someone opened the door, he yelled through chattering teeth, "He's frozen!"

After his father was lifted onto a gurney and wheeled away, Chap sped to the parking lot nearby, jumped out of the car, and staggered through the snow on numb feet.

Inside the emergency room, he stood at the counter, shaking visibly, vaguely aware of the stares from others in the waiting area—some with whiney toddlers on their laps, some holding sleeping babies on their shoulders, some with eyes darkened by pain.

"My father," he stammered as someone approached the other side of the counter. "He's frozen."

"So you brought him in," said a voice from above the pale blue uniform coat covered in small white snowmen with orange carrot noses, tall black hats, and mufflers of every color.

Chap stared. The snowmen began to blur, the colors all running together in sweeps and swirls. From very far away, he heard "His name?" before he crumpled to the floor.

* * *

The sounds were all wrong, so were the smells. Chap struggled to break through the fog to make sense of it all. Finally, his eyelids fluttered open, and he blinked in the light reflecting on the stark white walls. He was cocooned in blankets tucked tightly around his body. Near the pale green curtain which made the fourth wall of the narrow room was a chair with his damp coat and shoes on the seat and his wet socks draped over the back. Shapes moved beyond the drawn curtain on soles which made no noise. The only sounds were the squeak of a gurney on the tiled floor and hushed voices from places nearby. A large clock on the wall said 12:06. His sixteenth birthday was over.

The minute hand had inched to 12:25 before a face dominated by huge dark-rimmed glasses appeared around the curtain.

"Oh, I see you've joined us. Just call me Karen," the woman said as she briskly removed some of the blankets and wrapped a blood pressure cuff around his arm.

Chap remained still as she pumped it up and listened with the stethoscope. Then she stuck a thermometer into his mouth.

"My father," Chap said after she removed the thermometer.

"The doctors are working to warm him," she said.

She reached beneath the blankets to touch Chap's feet. "All toasty warm," she said, using words Chap doubted she'd learned in nurses' training.

Karen grinned, her big dark eyes lively behind the heavy glasses. "Looks like you're about back to normal, I'd say, if being a hero is normal for you."

"A hero?"

"You saved your father's life."

Chap tried to raise himself on wobbly arms but fell back.

"Whoa there," said Karen. "I said 'about normal.' Lie still while I raise the bed a little." As Chap slowly inched up, she added. "I'm guessing you're hungry. How about a midnight snack?"

Chap smiled weakly.

Ten minutes later, she returned with a huge bowl of steaming noodle soup, some crackers, a cup of hot tea, and a piece of apple pie. Chap was so hungry he almost forgot to thank her.

Then picking up a clipboard, she began to ask a lot of questions, the usual stuff at first, like their names, ages, and address.

"I found your student ID card in your coat but not your driver's license," she said. Chap's eyes widened, but she didn't notice. "Do they call you Charles or Chuck or Charlie?"

"Chap," he said.

"I'll bet there's a story there," she said, smiling.

Then she wanted to know what had happened to his father. Chap told her what he knew. He'd missed his father about 8:00, maybe 8:30—he hadn't looked at the clock. After searching the house from the basement to the attic, he'd found the footprints outside and followed them into the woods.

Chap added hastily, before she could ask, "I don't know when he left the house—or why, for that matter."

Karen continued to write a bit before she said, "Does he always wear four shirts?"

Before Chap could answer, a woman in a dazzling white jacket stepped through the curtain. Chap didn't look any higher than the name tag, which identified her as Dr. O'Shea.

After looking at the chart, she said, "Good. No ill effects from his time outside. And you're getting the information we need about the man."

"Is he all right?" Chap asked.

"He's stable and his body is warming, but we want to keep him overnight at least for observation. I'll need to talk with you again tomorrow. Karen will explain."

With that, Dr. O'Shea disappeared through the curtain.

"I need to ask you a few more questions before you leave," Karen said. "Have you noticed your father behaving in unusual ways recently—like wearing more than one shirt at a time?"

Chap hesitated, then said, "Yes."

"What exactly has he done?"

Suddenly, the words were spilling out—about the socks, the silence, the little paper squares, the wandering day and night, the calling for Lori.

"Who's Lori?" she asked.

"My older sister."

"Go on," she said softly.

But Chap felt out of words, too tired to explain his father's behavior anymore and not even sure he should be talking at all. What did four shirts and all these other questions have to do with getting him warm enough to go home?

Karen was looking at Chap, expecting more information it seemed. Noticing his coat lying on the chair, he asked for it. Reaching into the inside pocket, he took out the pages he'd torn from his journal weeks before.

"Here," he said, leaning back and closing his eyes.

Karen read for several minutes. Then she said, "Where is your sister?"

"She's in London."

"Oh," she said. It was quiet awhile before she looked up from the clipboard and added, "I think you need to tell her to come home."

"Why? I'm handling things," Chap said, his voice rising.

"I know," she said gently. "But not anymore. At least, not for now. I'll give you a number so your sister can contact Dr. O'Shea."

Chap stared at her, but she looked away.

"He's not all right, is he?"

She paused, then said, "It seems you've been the adult at your house, so I guess you deserve an adult answer. The doctor believes your father may be quite ill though it's very early to know for sure. Please call your sister. You will need her."

After helping him on with his coat and shoes, Karen walked him to the appointment desk. “You take care, Chap,” she said with a gentle touch to his cheek. “We’ll take care of your father for you tonight.”

Chapter 14

On January 19th, Chap had thought his worst problem was a father who'd forgotten his sixteenth birthday. But he wrong. At two in the morning on January 20th, he was sitting at the kitchen table, still cluttered with the homework he'd been doing. It seemed like days since he'd laid down his pencil to go search for his father, but in reality only five or six hours had passed. Chap stared at the wall, trying not to hear the creaks and groans of the old house, wanting to delay calling London for as long as possible.

Chap had felt so alone, even angry and resentful at times, as his father had become more and more withdrawn. But at that moment, when Chap was truly alone, he ached with missing his father, who didn't have to notice him or talk to him or even love him. He just needed to be there, not in a hospital bed miles away. The tiny red flowers on the wallpaper blurred.

A little before three o'clock, Chap dialed Lori's number, hoping he'd figured the time difference right, hoping she was already up. The idea of awakening her with the news he had seemed worse. When she answered the phone, his voice failed.

"Hello," she said again.

"Lori."

"Hey, Chap, is that you?"

"Yes," he said as tears slid down his cheeks.

"I'm so glad you called. Did your birthday present from me arrive? What did you two do to celebrate?"

Chap pictured her face, her brown eyes alive with happiness. In seconds, all that would change as her world would come crashing down. And it would be his fault—he'd been unable to take care of their father. He couldn't speak.

"Chap, why aren't you talking?" The tone of her voice changed. "Is something wrong?"

"I found him in the snow," Chap said with a sob.

Then he told Lori what had happened, stopping often when his voice broke. When he finished, he didn't have to ask her to come home.

"I need to go to work," she said, "but I'll contact the doctor and the airlines. I'll call you back later when I know more. You get some sleep now. Love you."

Chap climbed the stairs to his room, feeling bone-ache tired, maybe more tired than he'd ever been before. The lights he'd left on in each bedroom shone into the long hallway, but they did little to relieve the gloom. Without getting undressed, he crawled beneath the blankets on his bed, waiting to feel warm, wanting to feel safe, but the naked trees in the side yard cast dark shadows on the bedroom ceiling. He wanted to sleep. He needed to sleep. But he didn't sleep. The barely moving shadows failed to have a hypnotic effect as his mind raced through the jumble of the events of the past months, trying to make sense of it all.

As the eastern sky began to lighten, he closed his eyes.

* * *

Around noon, Chap once again drove to Riverwoods, slowly and carefully. The clinic, a three-story red brick building across the street from the hospital, was bustling with people. Too tired to climb even one flight of stairs, he stepped into the elevator with a mother, her face haggard, and three pale coughing children and a tiny frail man lost in a large wheelchair being maneuvered by his tiny frail wife.

After a nurse checked his temperature, pulse, and blood pressure, she ushered him into a small examination room where Dr. O'Shea sat, reading a file of papers. In the light of day, Chap looked beyond the white coat—all he'd noticed the night before—at the least doctor-looking doctor he'd ever seen with her short auburn hair spiked up and out, her ears sporting many earrings and her nose a tiny single blue gem. Any other day he'd have had to stifle an inappropriate smile, but that day her incongruous appearance, which might be expected at a teen hangout but certainly not at a clinic, seemed to fit with everything else that was unexpected, like the fact he was sitting in a clinic facing a doctor rather than in school facing a teacher.

Once Dr. O'Shea began asking even more questions about his father than Karen had in the emergency room, Chap felt so depressed there was no chance he'd smile.

"Does he have Alzheimer's?" he blurted out when Dr. O'Shea paused to finish some notes.

"So you know about that?" she said while sorting some papers. Then she closed the file and placed her hands on top, fingers laced. "To answer your question, Alzheimer's cannot be positively diagnosed before someone dies and the brain is autopsied. As a result, behavior is studied and some tests are given to try to rule out other forms of mental disease and to narrow in on Alzheimer's. That's the best we can do." She looked back at the file folder on her desk before adding, "A neurologist will see your father later today. I think it's likely his diagnosis will be Alzheimer's disease."

Chap said nothing. He just stared.

When Dr. O'Shea asked if his sister was coming home, Chap nodded.

"I'd like to see you both here day after tomorrow," she said. "I think we'll know more then."

Dr. O'Shea looked at him, her face relaxing and her voice becoming less brisk. "I can only imagine what you've been feeling. No matter what he's done, try to remember he's had little or no control over his actions—maybe for the past several years. Many people suffering from Alzheimer's are so frustrated with their inability to function and communicate that they lash out in anger."

Chap dropped his eyes, no longer able to meet her gaze.

"Remember the man you knew years ago," she said softly, reaching over to touch his hand before she left the room.

The nurse reappeared and took him to the appointment desk.

* * *

Chap saw his father in the hospital bed, as pale and still as when Chap had found him in the snow. But his hand was warm to the touch. His father didn't open his eyes— even when Chap said that Lori would be coming soon.

* * *

Leaving the hospital, Chap drove to the college campus, circling several blocks until he found a space that didn't require parallel parking. Then he walked to the little restaurant where he and Erica had gone together and slid into a booth, but it wasn't the same alone. Nothing was the same alone. He finished a cup of raspberry herbal tea but left before ordering anything to eat.

In less than twelve hours, Lori's plane would be landing in Indianapolis, but the thought of spending even that amount of time alone in the big empty house was unbearable. Chap wandered around the campus awhile before heading to the high school. The buses were pulling out as he parked far back on the lot.

Before entering the building, Chap pulled up the hood on his coat. It would be definitely unwise to run into Mr. Mueller since Chap had called himself in sick.

When Chap entered Mrs. Hunt's room, she said with a smile, "You're looking pretty healthy for someone on the absence list today."

"Busted, huh?" he said. "Actually, I was with my father at the hospital until after midnight."

"I'm sorry. What happened?"

"He got lost in the snow, and I didn't find him for hours. I'm not exactly sick, but I'm not exactly playing hooky either. My sister's flying home late tonight, so I don't know when I'll get back to school for sure."

They talked a little while about what Chap had missed and what the class would be doing next. She asked a few questions about his father and Lori, whom she remembered from years before.

As she started to fill a large white canvas bag with papers and books, Chap headed towards the door. He was almost there when she said, "How did you get here anyway?"

"I drove," he said without turning around.

"Oh, and that would be without a license, I'd say."

He said nothing.

"Chap, you aren't going to drive to Indianapolis?"

"Oh, no," he said. "I think Lori's words included 'grounded for life.'"

"But I'm right about you having no license?"

Chap turned around to face her, trying to meet the gray eyes that peered at him over the half glasses. He didn't answer.

"It's okay to ask for help," she said softly. "It seems to me you've handled quite enough already."

Dropping her dark green grade book into the bag, she stepped to a student desk to pick up her coat lying there.

"I have a plan," she said.

Chap said nothing.

"My guess is you're hungry."

Chap smiled. "Everyone seems to think that," he said, remembering the midnight snack in the emergency room

"So how about I treat you to a pizza—and then take you home."

"Oh, no, I can drive," he said quickly, refusing the ride but not the pizza.

"I know you can. You didn't fly here," she said with a smile. "But the point is I've got a problem. If I let you drive when I know you're illegal, I could get in trouble. I know I complain about you guys, but I rather do like my job."

Chap didn't know what to say.

Mrs. Hunt continued, as she started for the door, "I'll drive your car off the school lot since it's not registered to be here. I've got a friend who lives a couple of blocks over. We'll leave it there. Then we'll walk back here and take my car. Lori can get your car later. I assume she'll have to return a rental."

Mrs. Hunt paused to look directly at Chap. "How's that for a plan?"

The words every kid in the school would've expected to come out of Chap's mouth didn't. Instead of saying, "Oh, no, I can't let you do that," he said, "Good plan."

* * *

At first, it seemed strange to be riding in a new silver-gray Nissan with an English teacher—Tom would have used a word like *weird* or *aberrant* or *unnatural*—but by the time they arrived at the pizzeria, Chap had told Mrs. Hunt more about his father and the latest about Erica's progress since the surgery. Then while they ate salads and waited for the pizza—they'd decided to try a Hawaiian mixture of mushrooms, pineapple, ham pieces, green peppers, and onions—she asked about his other sisters, whose names she remembered though she'd forgotten their birth order.

Then, without thinking, Chap said, "Do you have a family? Kids?"

He was immediately sorry as a pained expression flashed across her face.

"I didn't mean to pry," he said.

"I know you didn't. I guess some students are curious since I don't have any family stopping by the school."

She paused a bit before continuing. "I had a daughter, Jean Marie. She died suddenly at age five from an illness which rarely causes death. She was that statistical 'one in ten thousand.' Who thinks about the child who dies when so many don't?"

The pizza came—and it was easy to shift their attention to its wonderful aroma and taste.

After awhile, Mrs. Hunt finished answering Chap's question about her family—even though he hadn't asked again. She explained that her marriage had "limped along," as she called it, for another two years until she came home from her job at a bank one evening to find a good-bye letter propped up on the kitchen table.

"It was like a scene from a soap opera," she said, "but our divorce was amicable since all our emotions, good and bad, had died. After that, I went back to college to get my degree in English, and the rest is history."

They didn't talk much after that, but the silence was a comfortable one and the pizza was wonderful. Chap relaxed just a bit.

As they were finishing up the last of the pizza, Mrs. Hunt said, "I wish you'd asked for help, Chap. You've handled so much by yourself."

"I almost did—in my journal after Christmas."

"You changed your mind?"

"I wasn't sure what you'd do—what you'd have to do, I guess—if you knew."

"I know," she said. "Sometimes familiar bad things seem better than a possible change that's unknown."

She reached for her purse and the ticket lying on the table.

"Let me pay the tip," Chap said.

"You've got enough money?"

"Yes, but you don't want to know how I've been getting it," he said with a grin.

* * *

Chap was eating a very late snack or a very early breakfast—he didn't know what to call a peanut butter and jelly sandwich, a bag of chips, and an apple at 4:30 in the morning—when car lights from the lane flashed through the kitchen window. Without a coat, he raced down the back porch steps.

Suddenly, Lori was there, hugging him and looking at him and hugging him again. He didn't even try to hold back the tears. If real men don't cry, as Tom claimed, Chap sure had a long ways to go to earn that label.

* * *

The next day, it was Chap's turn to hold Lori as she sobbed in the hallway outside the hospital room where their father had given no sign that he recognized her.

* * *

When Chap and Lori went to see Dr. O'Shea, she introduced them to the neurologist—a Dr. something or other that ended in –ski, a tall thin man who looked every bit as doctorlike, complete with a stethoscope around his neck, as Dr. O'Shea didn't.

It was Lori's turn to answer questions and to describe their father's forgetfulness and his diminishing lack of interest in their activities and in conversation. The neurologist asked if any of his behavior before going out into the snow seemed dangerous to himself or others, and Chap again told about the fire in the house, the abandoned car, and the flooded kitchen. Lori stared in shocked silence.

Then Dr. O'Shea asked the question no one else had. "Has your father ever hit you?"

Lori said, "No," as Chap said, "Yes."

Lori's face blanched as she cried, "Oh, Chap, you didn't tell me."

Then she held his hand tight while he explained what at one point he'd wanted to tell Mrs. Hunt or Lori or anyone else who might've cared, but what now felt disrespectful said aloud, even to the doctors. His father hadn't meant to hurt him.

Finally, the questioning was done. The doctors conferred briefly in hushed tones. Then after apologizing for having other patients to see, Dr. Something-ski briskly shook their hands and left. Dr. O'Shea put down her pen and faced them.

"Based on what you both have told us and what the neurological exam has revealed, we believe your father is suffering from Alzheimer's disease," she said.

So now it had been said—Alzheimer's disease—for all to hear. She continued to explain how the disease was likely to progress, how Chap and Lori would not be able to care for their father with Chap in school and Lori working.

Chap hoped Lori was listening because he couldn't follow anymore. He was again trying to reconcile his father's behavior with the certain diagnosis that he was ill. Chap had thought his father was playing games, but all that time he was losing his mind to Alzheimer's.

Suddenly, Chap was too tired to deal with it all. And just as suddenly, he didn't have to.

Lori was home.

Chapter 15

It was barely light when Chap awoke. He laced his fingers behind his head and snuggled back down into his sleeping bag to watch the ceiling change from the pale gray of early dawn to light rose. Chap toyed with a metaphor—the changes in his life during the past months, the changing colors on the ceiling of his room. His life had certainly seemed gray enough before Lori had come home and sometimes afterward, but there had been some rosy times, too.

* * *

Time had flown once Lori got home. She was back, and she was once again in charge. But some things had seemed very gray.

When she returned to work at the office in Riverwoods, she said, "It's only a temporary transfer back here until you finish the school year. We'll move to Virginia in June."

When Chap protested, she said only, "My job is there."

Then she contacted a lawyer since she needed to become Chap's legal guardian and to have power of attorney for their father, who had been transferred from the hospital to a nursing home nearby. He had been awake most often when they went to see him but still silent and unresponsive.

* * *

Chap had gone back to school the week after finding his father in the snow to meet a really contrite Tom.

"Gee, man, why didn't you tell me you needed help?" he said.

"Thought I could handle things."

"Guess you did pretty good. He really wandered away in the snow? And you drove him to the hospital yourself?"

"He did. I did."

Tom seemed to think about that for a minute. "Really glad you're back in school," he said as he punched Chap on the arm for the first time in ages.

Even the punch felt pretty good.

* * *

Two weeks later, Tom was standing in the mayor's office by Lori when the mayor placed a medal on a wide blue ribbon around Chap's neck. Tom whooped as cameras flashed.

Those had been rosy times.

* * *

And so was Valentine's Day when Chap stepped into the kitchen after school to be greeted by the smell of apple pie.

Lori said with a smile, "I have a surprise."

"You're not being sent to London again, are you? That's where you ended up last time you baked an apple pie."

"Don't be silly," she said, flicking the dish towel at him.

"Wow, the good dishes—and a table cloth," he said, glancing at the table.

Then he paused. He might not be good at math, but even he recognized that three place settings was one more than he and Lori needed.

"Someone coming?"

"Could be," she said, the color rising in her cheeks. "Why don't you take your books upstairs and change clothes—maybe something a little more formal than a Colts sweatshirt." She gave him a little push towards the stairway. "And don't forget to use a comb."

"Nag, nag, nag," he said as he disappeared up the steps.

Chap heard the car as he was pulling on the new forest green sweater Lori had bought for him in northern England. After splashing water on his face and running a comb through his hair, he headed back downstairs.

As he stepped into the kitchen, the tall blond stranger standing beside Lori laughed out loud, making Chap wonder if he'd forgotten to zip his fly.

Before Chap could respond, the man stuck out his hand and said, with his mouth more serious but his eyes still laughing, "I'm sorry. That wasn't polite. But your sister has referred to you as 'my little brother' ever since I met her. I wasn't expecting a six-footer."

And that was how Chap met Douglas.

* * *

The next morning Chap awakened early. Douglas was sleeping in Marilee's room, which Lori had cleaned and made more presentable by removing the movie star pictures from the walls and the perfume bottles from the dresser top. After a quick shower, Chap pulled on the green sweater again and headed downstairs.

Lori was in the kitchen, laying strips of bacon in a large skillet. She looked radiant in a red sweater and jeans, her hair in dark curls around her face, her eyes gleaming.

"Well, what do you think?" she said.

"About what—the sunshine, your red sweater, the bacon—what?"

"Don't be dense," she shot back.

"Oh, you mean Douglas," he said, drawing out the name into two long syllables.

"Yes, I mean Douglas," she answered, giving him a punch as hard as Tom's.

Chap watched as the grease began to bubble up from around the rippled edges of the bacon slices. He was taking time to compose his words carefully.

Finally, he said, "Why didn't you tell me the real reason why we're not going to stay here—why we're moving?"

Chap waited as Lori turned over the sizzling bacon slices.

"Moving is never easy. They say the stress level is right up there with losing a close family member—and we've already done that." Her voice broke. She tightened her lips to get control before she continued. "I was afraid if you knew Douglas is the reason I want to move to Alexandria, you'd dislike him without ever getting a chance to know him."

She laid the fork down and turned to face Chap. "I didn't mean to lie to you—I was just afraid to tell you the whole truth. I knew Douglas was special the minute I met him in August. We wrote letters and talked a lot after I got sent to London, and he flew over for the Christmas holidays."

Lori looked back at the bacon, turning it once again. When she glanced back at Chap, her eyes were swimming in tears. "Please tell me you like him," she whispered.

"I like him," Chap said, opening his arms wide to give her a hug.

* * *

After a huge breakfast of pancakes, bacon, and fruit followed by leisurely conversation over several cups of tea, Douglas asked Chap to take him to the Church Rock he'd heard so much about.

They made the climb in silence, Chap in the lead. The day was crisp and clear with a fresh layer of snow making the view from the bluffs dazzling for this stranger who had come there. Sitting high above Wandering River, they talked about Douglas's family—he also had only sisters, two little ones—and his job with the company in Alexandria where Lori had worked with Mr. Burris. Chap told him about school and Tom and the track team. Chap found himself talking easily to Douglas, the same way he could talk to Erica and Lori. Chap didn't mind his questions, even the personal ones about Lori becoming his legal guardian and the changes that were coming.

"The guardian part is easy enough. Lori's taken care of me since before I can remember. She's my best friend. But the moving part—that's different. I've never lived anywhere but here." Chap stared at the river below. "But it hasn't seemed the same with our father away—even with Lori back. It feels like everyone else has left, so now it's our turn." Chap paused then added, "I just wish I could know ahead of time if any place else will ever feel like home."

They didn't talk for a while.

Finally, Douglas said, "I sure understand why you love this place."

Chap looked at his watch, then rose from the Church Rock. "Lori's expecting us back for lunch."

"Can you wait a minute?" Douglas said. "I need to talk to you about something else, and I don't quite know how to begin since I'm pretty new at this meet-the-family stuff."

Chap sat back down.

"I know I'm part of your problem—the moving part, that is—and I'm sorry for that."

Douglas looked down at the glittering Christmas-card picture below.

"I could tell you I'm going to ask for your permission to marry your sister, but that would be a lie. I intend to marry your sister—if she says yes—with or without your approval. I'm just really, really hoping you'll be on my side."

Chap glanced at Douglas—his finely chiseled nose and jaw, the windblown hair, and the clear blue eyes with the fine laugh lines around the corners. He thought of Lori's face with the high color in her cheeks and the sparkle in her eyes when she looked at Douglas. There wasn't any chance she'd say no.

"I'd like you to be my best man," Douglas said, rising. When Chap didn't answer right away, Douglas added, "Think about it."

They walked back to the house in silence.

In the kitchen, Douglas quickly slipped a diamond ring under Lori's sandwich as she looked for chips in the cupboard. When Douglas winked at Chap and put his finger to his lips, Chap knew he'd be the best man.

* * *

Then towards the end of February, both his life and the weather turned a dismal gray.

Chap reached for his journal which was lying on the floor next to a folded pair of clean khaki shorts, a red polo shirt, and his shoes. Except for the sleeping bag, the clothes, and the notebook, the room was totally bare. Chap turned to the journal entry he'd written the night before. It had taken over three months for him to get the words from his heart to the paper.

Saying good-bye should be simple enough. Someone is leaving, and someone is staying. They wave or hug or shake hands or kiss. Maybe one says, "See you later" or "Have a safe trip," and the other responds, "I'll call you when I get home." Then they don't see each other for days or months or even years, and they feel some degree of loss, even sadness, depending on who they are and how long they'll be apart. Even when it's the most final good-bye at a graveside, people know it's time. They must move away from the deep hole in the ground, leaving the flowers to wilt from the sun and the wind but taking the pain with them.

But I missed the time to say good-bye to my father.

For a long time, I didn't have a clue that it needed to be said. Then when the hints came that something was very, very wrong, I did the ostrich-with-head-in-the-sand routine. By the time the words I'd ignored in my head were said aloud, it was too late. There was no handshake or even a wave—we wouldn't have hugged or kissed anyway. And if I'd said, "See you later," before the wide, double doors of the VA hospital swung closed, it wouldn't have meant anything. It was too late. I wasn't able to tell my father good-bye because right before my eyes his mind had been stolen by Alzheimer's disease.

* * *

Chap hadn't cried in front of Lori during the long drive back from the VA hospital in Illinois to First Woods Road, but he'd cried that night when he was alone as droplets of cold winter rain ran down the window in his room.

***

A few weeks later, a realtor had pounded one "For Sale" sign into the slushy remains of a March snow fall at the foot of the lane and two others at either end of First Woods Road. As Chap and Lori waited for the house to sell, they began to sort through all the personal possessions from the attic to the basement, filling, labeling, and stacking box after box. Some stuff would be given away, some would be sold, a few personal items would be shipped to Julianna and Catherine—they hadn't been able to locate Marilee—and some would go with Chap and Lori to Virginia. In each room, they taped little signs on the furniture indicating what would be sold and what would be moved. They had avoided the door to the den, which had remained closed since January 19.

Finally, when the den was the last room to tackle, Lori announced in mid-April it would be their project the following Saturday.

Chap had been dreading the walk inside there for months. He hadn't told Lori about his late-night search of the room.

On Saturday morning, Lori said, as they cleared the breakfast dishes, "We'll want to save his manuscript, but we'll give away the books."

Chap said nothing as he wiped the kitchen table. Then he followed her to the den. But when she touched the door knob, he reached for her hand.

"Lori, don't."

"Don't what?"

"Don't go in."

She looked at Chap, her eyebrows raised. "Why not?" she said.

"You won't find a manuscript."

She stared.

"Because there isn't one."

Then Chap led her into the den to show her the pieces of paper which were stuffed into the drawers and the filing cabinet and sticking out of books and from under paperweights on the desk top. Most of the papers were covered in a large childish scrawl with names and places and dates and annotations—some related to their father's life, some to theirs, and some to his research for the book he'd never written. For years, their father had been trying to save what he knew before he lost it all.

Hour after hour, Lori and Chap stacked the papers in various piles, trying to sort them into some coherent order. But as noon approached, Lori worked slower and slower until finally she dropped onto the desk chair.

"We can't make sense of this, can we?" she said, her eyes sad as she looked around the room.

Chap didn't know what to say.

"Come on," she said, rising and taking his hand.

In the kitchen, they made sandwiches and filled a thermos with cocoa. Grabbing jackets and an old blanket from the basement, they headed for the clearing in the woods where the light filtered through the tiny new leaves above them. As they ate, they talked about their father, their sisters, the old house, the items in the boxes, the new life they would start soon many miles away. Saving things would not preserve the life they were leaving. Saving scraps of paper would not preserve their father. With the spring sunshine warming their backs, a sort of peace settled around them.

Back at the house, Chap and Lori filled box after box with their father's books. Then they carried sacks of paper scraps to the burning barrel. Later, through the kitchen window, Chap saw Lori standing there, watching the bits of glowing ash and smoke curl upwards as dusk faded into darkness.

* * *

As the morning sun cleared the tree tops, yellow light flooded Chap's room. Gray, rose, now yellow—the metaphor seemed to fail since Chap couldn't conceive of his life being a cheerful bright yellow any time soon. He sat up in the sleeping bag and stretched. Then he grabbed his clean clothes and headed for the shower.

A short time later, he quietly pulled the back door closed—a banana in one hand and some raisin toast clenched between his teeth. The dew-coated grass sparkled in the early morning sun as he headed towards the woods that bordered the high bluffs. He hadn't been to the Church Rock since going there with Douglas. And he would likely never go there again.

Wanting to hear the chirping of the birds which were busily setting up housekeeping or tending already finished nests, Chap removed the ear phones attached to the new iPod Tom and the guys had given him the last day of school. They'd surrounded him in the school parking lot and pushed him into Jason's old gray Toyota.

"Something to listen to besides Lori's voice," Tom had said as Chap pulled the iPod from the Radio Shack bag, adding a hasty "Just kidding" when Chap shot him a dirty look.

After Chap thanked the guys a bunch, he protested that he needed to get home.

"I knew you'd say that," Tom said as he pulled a scrap of paper from his pocket.

The note, written in Lori's handwriting, said, *Have a good time, Chap.*

Tom grinned the old self-satisfied, Tom-Sawyer grin. "We planned this together," he said. "Considered yourself kidnapped."

It had been a fun, rowdy evening at a local steak house, full of "remember when" stories and lots of steak, twice-baked potatoes, and huge hot yeast rolls slathered with homemade strawberry jam. The solemn handshakes all around afterwards and Tom's last words, "Seriously, Chap, we'll miss you," had challenged Chap's determination to stay light-hearted—and dry-eyed.

That was the second time he'd had to fight tears in one day—the other when Mrs. Hunt handed him her e-mail address with a note suggesting that he might like to continue their journal "conversations" long distance. Even though she hadn't said good-bye, they both knew it was.

* * *

Reaching the top of the bluffs, Chap sat down on the Church Rock. Honeysuckle vining around the undergrowth behind him perfumed the air. The familiar vista below was all decked out in fresh shades of green, the river high with late spring run-off, the birds flitting from tree to tree. A doe stepped warily from the woods and moved gracefully to the river to drink, followed moments later by a spotted fawn. Chap stared and stared—wanting to burn the scene into his memory.

The doe moved back into the trees, the fawn close behind her. The sun was high enough now to warm Chap's back. It would be a beautiful early June day.

Chap stood and stretched. Then he started down the faint path that followed the bluffs as they sloped down to First Woods Road. He paused by a small clearing where his father had measured the ten-foot compass plant with his walking stick held straight o top of his head. Nothing there was nearly that tall in June.

The path ended at a point about midway between the Andersons' cabin and the Smiths' house. Chap looked north towards the cabin, but he wouldn't go there. Instead, he headed south. Soon he was jogging easily, evidence of his training for track which had resulted in a number of ribbons, now tucked into one of his to-be-moved boxes along with the photo album and the letters from the trunk in the attic, his mother's Christmas tree ornaments, and his worn brown teddy bear.

When he reached their mail box, he looked up the lane at the big white house, the yard he'd mowed for the last time, and the chrysanthemums already tall and green. Except for the rented yellow moving van with Lori's little car chained up behind it, everything seemed so familiar.

A bright yellow truck, he thought as he remembered the sunshine on the ceiling of his room. Maybe the metaphor did work. Maybe the yellow truck foreshadowed good things to come.

He pictured the house with the three little boys who'd be moving in soon running upstairs and down, inside and out—the house with the window shades up, sunlight in all the rooms, new flowers in the pots on the front steps, and voices calling from room to room. He wondered if anyone would notice the place on the downstairs bedroom door frame where his father had charted their heights each January first—Chap's line inching up to finally pass all his sisters' lines. He wondered if books would fill his father's den and which boy would watch sunrises from his bedroom window. Chap wondered if they would find the Church Rock and gaze at Wandering River from high up. He wondered if one of them would discover the heron.

With his heart beating hard, Chap opened the mail box, hoping for a letter addressed to him and finding one. Sliding it into his back pocket, he walked on south. There was one more place he wanted to go.

The woods were noisy with bird calls and chirps. Squirrels scampered from tree to tree, and a rabbit darted deeper into the woods as he passed. When he got close to the wooden bridge, he moved very slowly to the railing. Down at the first bend of the river, the heron was perched on a willow branch hanging down almost to the water. A heron—not a crane.

It was here he felt closest to Erica.

* * *

On the first Saturday in May, Lori had left early for a shopping trip in Riverwoods. Chap had slept in late for a change, throwing on an old pair of ragged cut-offs and a faded navy tee shirt before heading downstairs. He was just finishing a bowl of corn flakes when he saw a figure swing past the kitchen window. In seconds, there was a knock on the back door and a face beaming at him through the glass. He flung open the door and stared.

"Am I going to have to go through this again?"

He stared.

"Are you mute?" she said with a grin.

He stared.

"Do you know sign language?" she said, her grin widening.

He stared.

"How about this kind of sign language?' she said, propping her crutches against the doorframe and opening her arms wide.

He hugged her for a long time.

* * *

The Andersons had come back for the weekend. Their house would be up for sale soon as well since they were returning to Chicago permanently.

Chap and Erica had talked and talked. They hadn't gone to the Church Rock since the distance and terrain were too difficult for Erica. They did, however, spend Sunday afternoon at the little clearing, hands touching as they shared the past few months.

Erica told about the surgeries which were over and the pain which was mostly gone.

"I want to walk without crutches," she said. "I want people to quit looking at me and thinking, Wonder what happened to her? All I need now is patience, but I'm not so good at being patient."

"I think you're good at everything," Chap said.

"You're sweet," she replied, wrinkling her nose at him.

Chap told her about Mrs. Hunt's last composition assignment which was related to the biographies the students had read. They each had written an interview between the subject of the biography and a modern reporter. Then in pairs, they'd presented the interviews to the class. Chap and Tom had worked together. Chap, wearing a dress and a bright cotton turban, played the role of Harriet Tubman while Tom read the reporter's questions. Then Chap was the reporter as Tom strode around dressed as P.T. Barnum.

Erica giggled.

Then she described the huge school she was now attending after having a tutor at home for two months. It was three times the size of Riverwoods High.

Chap told her all about Douglas and the plans for an outdoor wedding in September. Chap had decided he liked the idea of having a brother—even with the *in-law* part attached.

"I really like Lori," Erica said, "so I can't imagine not liking someone she loves."

Chap grinned at her.

"I mean Douglas, of course," she said in mock seriousness.

This time he wrinkled his nose at her.

Then all too soon their time together was over.

"I love you," he said before he kissed her. And then she was gone.

* * *

Chap watched the heron awhile longer. Then standing on the wooden bridge with the water gurgling over the rocks below, he took Erica's letter from his pocket. It was short. He read the last paragraphs over and over.

It's going to be hard to picture you in a city since my memories of you are so tied to the woods and the wooden bridge. I'll always treasure the closeness we had. I know that as we begin school next fall, we'll make new friends. But I wonder if any of mine will measure up to you.

I love you, Chap. Maybe someday we can cross the miles to meet again. Erica

Folding the letter gently, Chap whispered good-bye—to Erica, who was in Chicago, and to his father, who was lost to him.

The heron, however, was not lost. Chap would always be able to picture it returning from its annual migration to live along the banks of Wandering River amid the greens of spring and summer. The heron would be staying after he was gone.

About the Author

Jane S. Creason lives with her husband in a remodeled one-room schoolhouse, where she has lived since she was four years old. They have two adult children, both married, and four grandchildren. Jane earned her bachelor's and master's degrees at the University of Illinois. She has taught grade school, middle school, and high school and currently teaches English at a community college—all in East Central Illinois. Her hobbies include reading, working crossword puzzles, gardening, fishing with her husband, sewing, walking in the country, and spending time with their family and friends. Since Jane has lived in the same house with the same husband and taught English in the same county for much of her life, she describes herself as a contented Midwesterner who has put down serious roots.

About the Artist

David McLaughlin, Professor of Art Emeritus of Ohlone College at Fremont/Newark, California, founded and headed the college's Art Department in 1967. He taught painting, drawing, and art history there for thirty-five years. He did the cover artwork for *To Mount a Wind*, a book of poetry by Jane Creason's mother, Elizabeth Loeffler Swengel, and for *Plainston Chronicles, Volumes I and II,* a novel about the evolution of a unique educational system by Jane's father, Dr. Edwin M. Swengel. David is married to Jane's cousin, Penny Smith McLaughlin.